MATILDA HART

A Good Family
Matilda Hart
Copyright © 2025
Cover design by Mats Ingelborn
with illustrations from Midjourney
Author's portrait by Mego Studio
ISBN print: 978-91-90010-38-9
ISBN e-book: 978-91-90010-39-6
Published by Yabot AB, Sweden, 2026

Friday afternoon

The yard was too quiet. Ellie Carlson stood at the kitchen sink, water running over a half-rinsed tomato, staring through the glass. Lily had been there a moment ago, pushing her stuffed elephant on the swing. Now the swing moved empty in the breeze.

She could see the backyard, the gate in the fence that led to the walking path, the line of trees beyond that marked the edge of Heron Marsh Nature Preserve. Lily had been out there five minutes ago, singing one of her made-up songs.

Now the yard was empty. She opened the window.

"Lily?" Ellie's voice cracked. She cleared her throat and tried again. "Lily, come inside, please."

Nothing. Just the rustle of leaves, the distant hum of someone's lawn mower three houses down.

She set down the knife she'd been using to slice tomatoes and crossed to the back door, her bare feet soundless on the hardwood. The door stood half-open—she'd left it that way so she could hear if Lily called, so she could keep an eye on her while she made dinner.

Except she'd looked down at the cutting board for what, two minutes? Three?

"Lily!"

The swing moved gently in the breeze, Mr. Pemberton the elephant slumped against the chains. A cold spike in her chest. She pushed through the door and out onto the deck, scanning the yard, the fence line, the gate—

The gate—which Ellie had locked at noon, heaving her weight against the warped wood until the latch clicked—was wide open.

"No. No, no, no." She flew down the steps, across the grass. "Lily!"

The path beyond the gate stretched into shadow, lined with oak and pine. Anyone could be back there. Anything could happen in those woods, in that park where someone had seen the man—

"Mommy?"

Ellie spun. Lily stood by the corner of the house, her purple t-shirt grass-stained, her ponytail askew, grinning her gap-toothed smile.

"You didn't see me," she announced, beaming. "I was hiding."

The air rushed back into Ellie's lungs, harsh and stinging. She dropped to the grass, disregarding the wet stain blooming on her jeans, one hand pressed to her chest, the other reaching for her daughter.

"Come here. Come here right now."

Lily's smile faltered. She walked over, her sneakers dragging. "Are you mad?"

"No, baby. No." Ellie pulled her close, buried her face in Lily's hair—Play-Doh and peanut butter and something ineffably Lily, the scent that had defined Ellie's world for five years. "You just scared me. When I can't see you, you need to answer when I call, okay?"

"Okay." Lily's arms came around her neck, small and strong. "I was just playing."

"I know." Ellie kissed her forehead, her cheek, breathed her in one more time before letting go. "But we have to be careful right now. Remember what we talked about? About not going to the park alone?"

Lily nodded, her brown eyes solemn. At five, she didn't understand why she couldn't walk to the playground by herself anymore, why Ellie checked the locks on the doors twice every night, why the mothers at preschool pickup clustered together in tight groups, their voices low and urgent. She just knew something had changed, something that made her mother's smile brittle and her father's jaw tight when he thought no one was looking.

"Can I watch TV?" Lily asked.

"Half an hour. We're having guests for dinner, remember?"

Lily brightened—she loved having people over—and skipped toward the house. Ellie followed more slowly, closing the gate, checking the latch. Her hands shook as she fastened it. She pressed her palms together, willing them to be still.

This had to stop. This fear that lived under her skin. Lily was fine. She was right there, safe, probably already sprawled on the living room couch watching some cartoon about talking animals.

But as Ellie climbed the deck steps and went back inside, she couldn't shake the image of that open gate, that empty yard, those three or four minutes when she hadn't known where her daughter was.

The tomatoes sat on the cutting board, half-sliced.

She picked up the knife and tried to focus on the simple task—slice, scoop, arrange on the plate.

Her phone sat face-up beside the sink, the screen dark. She glanced at it, then looked away, then gave in and picked it up.

She checked her phone. A new notification from the Nextdoor app.

Sighting: Heron Marsh entrance. 4:40 PM.

Gray hoodie.

Ellie looked at the digital clock on the oven. 4:40 PM was an hour ago. The Marsh entrance was a three-minute walk from her back fence.

She put the phone face-down and returned to the tomatoes. The knife felt slippery in her hand.

The predator—that's what people were calling him, though the police hadn't used that word in any official statement. Just "a person of interest" in what they termed "inappropriate approaches toward minors." Three incidents now, maybe four, depending on which version you believed. A man in a gray hoodie and sunglasses approaching children at the park, offering candy, asking them to help find his lost dog. So far, thank God, the children had all run away or screamed or found their parents.

And he was here, in Willow Pond, in their neighborhood, walking past playgrounds, watching children play.

Ellie finished the tomatoes and started on the mozzarella, her movements mechanical. She'd invited Marcus Webb and Derek and Chelsea Thornton for dinner—a small Friday night gathering, nothing fancy.

	

Ben would be home any minute. She should make the salad dressing, check on the chicken in the oven, set the table.

She should stop thinking about gray hoodies and open gates and the hundred ways a child could vanish.

Car tires crunched on gravel outside—the driveway. She glanced at the clock: 5:47. Ben was late, but not by much. She heard the car door, then nothing for a long moment. When the front door finally opened, she called out, "We're in here."

Lily's shriek of delight echoed from the living room. "Daddy!"

Ben dropped his briefcase. "Hey, bug. What are you watching?"

Ellie rinsed her hands and dried them on a towel, then went to the doorway between the kitchen and living room. Ben stood by the couch, his suit jacket slung over one arm, his tie loosened, his sandy brown hair mussed from the wind or from running his hands through it—a habit he'd developed lately, usually when he was on the phone with someone from work.

"Long day?" she asked.

He looked up, and for just a moment she saw something in his face—exhaustion, yes, but also strain, a tightness around his eyes that hadn't been there a month ago. Then he smiled, and it was Ben again, her Ben, the man who'd proposed to her on a beach in Maine nine years ago, who'd held her hand through twenty-two hours of labor, who built elaborate block towers with their daughter every Saturday morning.

"Not too bad." He crossed to her and kissed her, his hand warm on her waist. "Something smells good."

"Lemon chicken. And Marcus is bringing dessert, so don't get your hopes up for my brownies."

He laughed. "Marcus and his fancy pastries. I can't compete with that."

"No one can." She studied his face, trying to read what she'd seen there a moment ago. "Everything okay at work?"

"Fine. Just the usual end-of-quarter chaos." He set his jacket on the back of a chair and loosened his tie another inch. "Are we doing drinks before dinner?"

"If you want. People should start arriving around six-thirty."

He nodded and headed upstairs, his footsteps heavy on the treads. Ellie watched him go, that flicker of unease still present, still unexplained. Ben had been working late more often these past few weeks, coming home distracted, checking his phone at odd hours. When she'd asked about it, he'd mentioned the VP position—a promotion he and Derek Thornton were both competing for. The decision was coming next week.

That explained the stress. It explained everything.

Except it didn't explain why, when she'd hugged him just now, he pulled away too quickly. It was subtle—a shift in weight, a glance over her shoulder at his phone buzzing on the counter—but it was there. The Ben of a month ago wouldn't have let go until she did.

She shook her head and went back to the kitchen. The chicken was golden and fragrant when she pulled it from the oven. She set it on the stove to rest and checked her phone one more time.

No new posts about the man in the gray hoodie.

No new sightings.

But that didn't mean he was gone. It just meant no one had seen him.

Yet.

She looked out the window one last time. The wind had died down, but the swing was still moving. And down by the fence, where the shadows stretched long and dark, the gate was unlatched again.

CHAPTER 2

Friday evening

Ellie adjusted the hydrangeas for the third time, forcing a bloom into the center to hide a gap in the arrangement. Perfect surface, rotting stems. Just like tonight needed to be. When the doorbell rang at seven sharp, she wiped her damp palms on her apron before reaching for the handle.

"You look beautiful," Marcus said, handing her a bottle of wine and a small bouquet of white roses. "These made me think of you."

"Marcus, you didn't have to—"

"I wanted to." His smile was warm, genuine. At forty-seven, Marcus had the kind of face that suggested he'd spent more time reading than worrying, with silver threading through his dark hair and laugh lines around intelligent gray eyes.

Behind him, a white Range Rover pulled into the driveway. Derek and Chelsea Thornton emerged, Chelsea in a designer dress that probably cost more than Ellie's entire outfit, Derek in casual slacks and a pale blue shirt that looked deceptively simple but screamed expense.

"Ellie!" Chelsea air-kissed both her cheeks, bringing with her a cloud of perfume. "Your hydrangeas look amazing. I simply cannot get mine to bloom like that."

"It's just Miracle-Gro," Ellie said, stepping aside to let them in.

Derek shook her hand, his grip firm and confident.

"Something smells incredible. You're making us all look bad, Ellie."

"Ben's in the living room," she said, gesturing toward the room where classical notes spilled from the piano. "Can I get anyone drinks?"

She escaped to the kitchen, grateful for a moment alone. Through the doorway, she could hear the men greeting each other—Ben's voice lighter than it had been earlier, Derek's booming laugh. Marcus said something she couldn't make out, and they all chuckled.

In the living room, Marcus rose from the piano bench—he'd been playing something soft and melancholy.

"That was beautiful," Ellie said. "What is it?"

"Chopin. Nocturne in E-flat major." He smiled, but there was something wistful in it. "My mother used to play it."

Chelsea swirled her Pinot, studying the room with an appraiser's eye. Derek stood by the fireplace, one hand in his pocket, studying the family photos on the mantel.

Derek lifted the framed photo from the mantel. "Is this Lily?"

"Last summer," Ben said. "She lost her two front teeth the week before we left. Insisted on eating corn on the cob anyway."

"She's adorable," Chelsea said. "You're so lucky, Ellie. Five is such a sweet age."

"Most days," Ellie said with a laugh. "Other days she's a tiny dictator."

Derek's phone buzzed. He glanced at the screen,

then at Chelsea, some silent communication passing between them. Chelsea's smile didn't waver, but something flickered behind her eyes—nervousness, maybe, or anticipation.

Ellie filed it away without knowing why.

"Speaking of which, where is the little empress?" Marcus asked.

"Asleep, thank God. She fought bedtime like I was sending her to the gulag, but she finally went down."

Ellie excused herself to check on dinner. In the kitchen, she basted the chicken, stirred the potatoes, checked the green beans. Her hands moved through familiar motions while her mind wandered. Through the doorway, she could see Ben talking to Derek, both men laughing at something. They looked like friends. They were friends—or had been, before this VP position turned them into competitors.

She heard Derek say something about Thursday, about the board meeting. Ben's smile tightened at the corners.

When she returned with appetizers—a cheese board she'd assembled with more care than she wanted to admit—soft jazz was playing from the Bluetooth speaker, something Ben must have started while she was gone. The conversation had shifted to the neighborhood, to property values, to the new townhouse development going up where the old dairy farm used to be.

"I think it's sad," Ellie said. "All that open space, just gone."

"Progress," Derek said with a shrug. "People need places to live."

"People need green space too," Marcus countered. "Not everything has to be developed."

"Says the man with a three-acre lot in Newton," Derek shot back, but he was smiling.

"Guilty," Marcus admitted. "Though I inherited it, for what that's worth."

Chelsea turned to Ellie. "Speaking of the neighborhood, did you see the Nextdoor post today? Someone spotted that creep again. Near the elementary school this time."

The temperature in the room seemed to drop. Ellie's stomach clenched.

"What creep?" Marcus asked.

"There's been someone hanging around," Ben said quietly. "Approaching kids near Heron Marsh. Police haven't caught him yet."

"I heard he actually touched a girl at Heron Marsh— grabbed her arm before she screamed," Chelsea said, taking a sip of wine. Her eyes were bright, excited—but there was something else there too, something calculated that made Ellie shift uncomfortably. "They say he drives a white van, or maybe a gray sedan. Though honestly, that description could fit half the men in town. It's the behavior pattern that's really distinctive."

Ellie's hand went to her throat. "Lily plays at Heron Marsh."

"Let's not—" Ben started.

"No, we should talk about it," Derek interrupted. "Everyone needs to be vigilant. These predators, they count on people being complacent."

"The police are investigating," Ben said. "I'm sure they'll catch whoever it is soon."

"Maybe." Derek took a sip of wine. "But in the meantime, we all need to be careful. Chelsea and I are thinking of getting a security system. Cameras on the doors, motion sensors, the whole thing."

"We already have a video doorbell," Ellie said. "And we keep the gate locked."

"The police should talk to people who work with troubled individuals," Chelsea said, swirling her wine thoughtfully. "Crisis counselors, therapists—they see these patterns all the time. Specific behavioral signatures." She glanced at Derek, some unspoken communication passing between them. "Someone could probably describe exactly how a predator like that would operate, down to the smallest detail."

Derek nodded slowly, as if considering this for the first time, though something in his expression suggested otherwise.

"Good," Chelsea said, patting her hand. "You can't be too careful these days."

Ellie stood. "Dinner's ready. Should we move to the table?"

The dining room flickered in the candlelight of Ellie's grandmother's silver taper holders. She had set the table with military precision—forks aligned, napkins starched—an armor against the evening's undercurrents.

For ten minutes, they sustained the illusion of a friendly gathering. Marcus told self-deprecating stories about his botched trip to Vermont, while Chelsea critiqued the new textured wallpaper in the powder room.

"It's bold," Chelsea said, pushing a green bean around her plate. "I usually advise clients to go lighter in small spaces. But good for you for taking a risk."

"Risk is necessary," Derek said. He sliced into his chicken, the knife screeching briefly against the china. The sound made Ellie wince. "Isn't that right, Ben? Patterson sent that memo out this morning about the quarterly projections. High risk, high reward."

The table went quiet. The smooth jazz from the other room seemed suddenly loud.

"I saw the email," Ben said, reaching for his water glass. His knuckles were white. "I'll have the analysis ready for the board meeting."

"Thursday, right?" Derek smiled, but his eyes remained flat, assessing. "I already sent mine over. Patterson seemed... concerned about the delays in your department."

"There are no delays," Ben said, his voice tight. "Just thoroughness."

"Of course." Derek raised his glass in a mock toast. "Quality over speed. A noble strategy. Let's hope the board agrees."

Chelsea's hand found Derek's, her fingers tightening possessively. "Derek's worked so hard for this. We've worked so hard." Her smile at Ellie was still warm, but there was something brittle beneath it, like ice over deep water. "I'm sure you understand how important it is."

Ellie looked at Marcus, silently begging for an intervention.

"This chicken," Marcus announced loudly, "is extraordinary. Ellie, is there lemon in the marinade?"

The tension didn't break, but it stretched thin enough to breathe again. Yet as Ellie watched Derek chew, she realized this wasn't just friendly competition. Derek wasn't here to have dinner. He was here to inspect the carcass before the kill.

After the main course, Marcus asked if anyone minded if he played the piano.

"Please," Ellie said. "I love when you play."

He moved to the bench, his long fingers finding the keys with ease. The music that poured out was something classical, something Ellie didn't recognize but that made her chest feel full and tight at the same time.

Chelsea leaned against Derek, his arm around her shoulders. Ben reached under the table and squeezed Ellie's hand.

For a moment, everything felt perfect.

Then the doorbell rang.

Ellie glanced at Ben, who shrugged. "I'll get it," she said.

Through the front door's sidelight, she could see a figure on the porch—male, thin, familiar in a way that made her stomach sink.

She opened the door a crack. "Will."

Her cousin stood there in a rumpled jacket, his hair greasy, his eyes bloodshot. He smiled, but it didn't reach his eyes.

"Hey, cuz." His breath smelled sour, stale. "Sorry to interrupt. I just need a quick word."

"We have guests," Ellie said. "This isn't a good time."

"It never is, though, is it?" He pushed against the door, trying to step into the foyer.

Ellie held firm. "Will, please—"

"Five minutes. That's all I need." His voice rose, took on a wheedling quality. "I'm in a jam, Ellie. A real jam this time. Just let me in and we can—"

She heard footsteps behind her. Ben appeared at her shoulder, his body filling the doorframe, physically blocking Will's path.

"You need to leave," Ben said. His voice was flat, cold.

"Hey, Ben, good to see you too." Will's smile turned ugly. "I was just asking my favorite cousin for a little help. Family helps family, right?"

"How much?" Ellie asked, just wanting this over with.

"Ellie—" Ben started.

"How much, Will?"

"Five hundred would get me sorted."

"I don't have that kind of cash in the house."

Will's eyes darted past her, toward the dining room, toward the murmur of voices as their guests tried to pretend they couldn't hear this humiliating scene playing out in the hallway. "Come on, cuz. You live in this big house, you've got all this—"

"Wait here." Ellie grabbed her purse from the hall table and pulled out her wallet. She had a hundred and forty dollars—the emergency cash she kept for the babysitter, for unexpected expenses. She handed it all to him, every bill.

Will counted it, his face twisting. "This is it?"

"That's everything I have. Cash only. And then you need to go, and you can't come back here asking for more."

He flashed a grin that showed too much gum. "You're a saint, Saint Ellie."

He backed down the porch steps, gave a mocking salute, and disappeared into the darkness.

Ellie closed the door and leaned against it. Her hands were trembling. The empty wallet felt wrong in her grip, lighter than it should be.

"I'm sorry," she whispered.

Ben pulled her into his arms. "Not your fault. Not your responsibility."

"He's family."

"He's a leech." Ben's voice was harder than she'd ever heard it. "Next time he shows up, we call the police."

She nodded against his chest, but she knew there wouldn't be a next time. Will always knew exactly when he'd pushed too far.

When they returned to the dining room, everyone pretended nothing had happened. Marcus offered to pour more wine. Chelsea started a story about a disastrous open house she'd attended.

But the evening's magic had broken.

By ten o'clock, everyone had made their excuses and left. Chelsea hugged Ellie and whispered, "Call me if you need anything," in a way that suggested she'd heard everything. Derek shook Ben's hand. Marcus was the last to leave, pausing at the door to say, "If you need anything, Ellie. I mean it."

"I know," she said. "Thank you."

* * *

The guests departed in a trickle of awkward goodbyes. Through the bay window, Ellie watched the taillights of Thornton's white Range Rover, followed by Marcus's Volvo, pausing at the stop sign longer than necessary before turning toward Newton.

The house felt enormous in their absence.

Ben locked the front door and tested the handle twice. Ellie stood in the foyer, surrounded by the wreckage of the evening—wine glasses balanced on every surface, crumpled cocktail napkins, Chelsea's lipstick print on a water glass like evidence of a crime.

"That went well," Ben said. The silence that followed swallowed his words whole.

Ellie didn't respond. She bent to pick up Lily's stuffed elephant, Mr. Pemberton, from where he'd been abandoned near the stairs. The elephant's button eye caught the light.

"Will's got a problem." Ben's voice had gone tight. "A serious problem."

"I know."

"Showing up here like that—" He stopped himself, ran both hands through his hair. When he looked at her, his eyes were ringed with exhaustion. "You can't keep giving him money."

"I gave him a hundred and forty dollars."

"It won't stop. You know that."

She did know. Will had been circling closer for months—first the occasional text, then the voicemails, then the showing up. Each time, the desperation had deepened. Each time, she'd told herself it would be the last.

"Derek was a real piece of work tonight," she said.

Ben's jaw worked. "Derek's always been a piece of work."

"He thinks he's already got the VP position."

"Derek thinks a lot of things." Ben moved past her toward the kitchen, started loading the dishwasher with mechanical precision. "Doesn't mean they're true."

Ellie followed him, began gathering dessert plates. The chocolate cake sat half-eaten, Chelsea's slice barely touched—she'd mentioned a cleanse three times during dinner. "You said the announcement was Thursday. The board meeting."

"That's right."

"So next week."

"Next week." He didn't look at her, just kept loading glasses one by one, his movements careful, controlled.

She wanted to push, to ask why he'd been so late coming home, why Derek had seemed so confident, why Ben looked like he hadn't slept in a week. But something in the set of his shoulders stopped her.

They worked in silence, the only sound the clink of dishes and the distant hum of the refrigerator. Through the kitchen window, Ellie could see the backyard dissolving into darkness. The gate was closed now—Ben had checked it twice after finding it unlatched earlier.

When the kitchen was clean, they climbed the stairs together. Ben paused at Lily's door, eased it open. Their daughter slept on her back, arms flung wide, Mr. Pemberton tucked under one elbow. The nightlight shaped like a crescent moon cast soft shadows across her face.

"She's perfect," Ellie whispered.

Ben slipped an arm around her waist, pulled her close. For a moment they stood together in the doorway, watching Lily breathe. This was the image Ellie wanted to freeze—the three of them safe, together, insulated from the world outside.

But then she remembered Chelsea's voice at dinner: *"They say he approaches them near the playground. Offers them candy, asks if they want to see his dog. Classic predator behavior."* And Derek's response: *"If I had kids, I wouldn't let them out of my sight. Not in this neighborhood. Not anymore."*

The words had been aimed at Ben and Ellie, a subtle accusation of negligence.

She felt Ben's lips against her temple. "Come to bed."

They retreated to their room. Ben disappeared into the bathroom while Ellie changed into pajamas, her fingers clumsy on the buttons. She heard water running, the electric toothbrush, the medicine cabinet clicking shut.

When he emerged, he was already half-asleep on his feet. He climbed into bed and was unconscious within minutes, his breathing evening out into the deep rhythm she'd known for twelve years.

Ellie lay beside him in the dark, staring at the ceiling.

The house settled around them with its familiar creaks and sighs. The furnace kicked on. Somewhere downstairs, the ice maker rattled. Normal sounds. Safe sounds.

But she couldn't sleep.

Her mind kept circling back to Will on the front porch, to Derek's knowing smile, to the open gate, to the news story she'd read that morning while Ben was in the shower—another incident at Heron Marsh, this time a seven-year-old girl who'd been followed from the playground. The girl had run, thank God. The man had vanished into the trees.

Ellie turned onto her side, watched the red numbers on the alarm clock flip from 12:47 to 12:48.

She thought about getting up, going downstairs to check the doors again. But what would that solve? Ben had already locked them. She'd watched him do it.

She reached for her phone on the nightstand, wanting to check the Nextdoor app—had anyone posted about the gray sedan?—but her hand found only the smooth wood surface. She must have left it in the kitchen during cleanup. The sleeping pill was already softening the edges of her thoughts, making it hard to remember.

It could wait until morning.

Ellie pressed her palms against her eyes until she saw stars. She was being paranoid. She knew that. The odds of anything actually happening to Lily were astronomically small—she'd read the statistics, knew that most child abductions were committed by family members, that stranger danger was largely a media-fueled panic.

But knowing the statistics didn't help. Not when

she'd seen that open gate. Not when she could so easily imagine Lily wandering through it, lured by a voice calling from the trees, a promise of something wonderful just out of sight.

Beside her, Ben made a sound in his sleep—half sigh, half moan. His face was turned away from her, one arm thrown across the pillow where she should have been lying.

She studied the back of his neck, the vulnerable curve of his spine beneath the T-shirt. He was the man who remembered her coffee order after twelve years, who still left notes in her coat pockets, who cried at Lily's preschool graduation.

He was also the man who'd been late on Wednesday. Who'd said there was a meeting, that it had run long. But what if—

No.

She shut down the thought before it could complete itself. This was what the fear did—it burrowed into everything, poisoned everything. She'd watched it happen to other mothers at Little Sprouts, the way their anxiety metastasized until they saw threats everywhere, trusted no one.

She wouldn't let that happen to her.

Ellie closed her eyes, forced her breathing to slow. She counted backward from one hundred, a meditation technique her mother had taught her. By seventy-three, her thoughts had begun to blur. By sixty-one, she was drifting.

She was almost asleep when she heard it.

A sound downstairs. Soft but distinct.

The click of a latch.

Her eyes snapped open. Her body went rigid, every muscle locking into place. She held her breath, listening.

Nothing. Just the house, settling. Just her imagination.

But then it came again. Not a latch this time—footsteps. Careful, deliberate footsteps moving across the kitchen floor.

Ellie's heart kicked into high gear. She turned to wake Ben, her hand already reaching for his shoulder—

And stopped.

Because what if she was wrong? What if it was nothing, and she woke him for the third time this week over phantom sounds? He needed sleep. He had the board meeting next week. She couldn't keep doing this to him.

She sat up slowly, listening.

The footsteps had stopped.

Probably just the refrigerator, she told herself. Or the dishwasher cycling to a new phase. Or the house contracting as the temperature dropped. Houses made noise. Their house was only fifteen years old, but it still counted as old in a development like Willow Pond, where everything was fresh and raw and still settling into itself.

She was being ridiculous.

But she was already out of bed, her feet finding her slippers in the dark. She pulled on her robe and moved to the door, eased it open without letting the hinges creak.

The hallway was dark except for the nightlight plugged in near Lily's room. Ellie paused at her daughter's door, listened to her breathe. Still asleep. Still safe.

She continued to the stairs, one hand on the railing. The steps were carpeted, muffling her descent. At the bottom, she paused again, scanning the living room. Everything looked normal—furniture in place, front door still locked, deadbolt engaged.

The kitchen was dark. She flipped the light switch.

Empty. Clean. Exactly as they'd left it.

Ellie moved to the back door, tested the handle. Locked. She peered through the window into the backyard. The security light mounted above the garage illuminated the lawn, the swing set, the fence line.

The gate was closed.

She let out a breath she hadn't known she was holding.

See? Nothing. Just her mind playing tricks, inventing threats where none existed.

She turned to head back upstairs—

And saw it.

On the kitchen counter, beside the fruit bowl: her phone. Not where she'd assumed she'd left it. But it was something else that made her stop.

The phone wasn't dark. It was lit up, showing her lock screen—a photo of Lily at the beach last summer, grinning gap-toothed at the camera.

Ellie picked it up. No new notifications.

It was warm. Not cold like the granite countertop, but warm, as if it had been held recently. As if someone had been using it moments before she walked in.

She unlocked the phone, checked her recent apps.

Nothing unusual. No apps open that she hadn't used. The last thing she'd looked at was a recipe site, hours ago, while preparing dinner.

But the warmth. The position. Both were wrong.

Unless they weren't. She'd been holding the phone while she cooked—maybe the batteries were running hot from use. Maybe she had put it next to the fruit bowl while cleaning up after dinner and simply forgotten.

The sleeping pill. It made everything fuzzy, smeared the edges of her memory until she couldn't trust what she knew.

She pressed her palm to her forehead. She couldn't trust her own memory anymore. The stress, the fear, the constant vigilance—it was eating away at her sense of reality.

Ellie set the phone down and backed away from the counter. She was either losing her mind, or someone had been in her house.

She didn't know which possibility frightened her more.

She climbed the stairs again, her legs heavy with adrenaline that had nowhere to go. At the top, she stopped. She couldn't go back to bed. She couldn't lie there in the dark, waiting.

Instead, she lowered herself to the floor at the top of the stairs, her back against the wall, her eyes fixed on the darkness below. From here, she could see anyone who came up. She could hear Lily's door if it opened.

She sat there, watching, until the first gray light of dawn crept through the windows.

CHAPTER 3

Saturday morning

The morning arrived, announced by Lily jumping on their bed at six-forty-five.

"Pancakes!" she shouted. "Saturday pancakes!"

Ellie forced her eyes open, every muscle protesting. She'd only left her post at the top of the stairs twenty minutes ago, slipping back into bed before anyone could find her there.

Ben groaned and pulled the pillow over his head. He looked terrible—skin pale, dark circles under his eyes.

"I'll handle the pancakes," he said.

She didn't move.

By the time she came downstairs, dressed in jeans and an old sweatshirt, Lily was at the kitchen table with her coloring book.

"I have to run into the office for a few hours," Ben said, draining half his coffee in one go. "There's a problem with the Vertex data that can't wait until Monday."

"On Saturday?"

"I know. I'm sorry. I'll be back by lunch."

After he left, Ellie stood at the kitchen window and watched his car disappear down Meadow Lane.

At ten-thirty, the doorbell rang.

Through the front window, she could see Derek's BMW in the driveway.

"I'll be right back," she told Lily. "Stay here."

She opened the door to find Derek on the porch, dressed in tennis whites, holding a plastic bag.

"Morning, Ellie!" His smile was too bright. "Sorry to drop by unannounced. I realized after I got home last night that Ben lent me a wrench a few weeks ago and I never returned it. Plus, I still have his workshop key from when I borrowed the table saw last month. Thought I'd bring everything back while I was in the neighborhood."

Ellie stared at the bag. "Ben's not here."

"Oh?" Derek's eyebrows rose with theatrical surprise. "I tried his cell, but no answer. He's not sick, is he?"

"He's at the office."

"On Saturday? That's dedication." Derek's smile widened. "Though I guess we're all putting in extra hours these days. Big week coming up."

"Right. The board meeting."

"Thursday, yeah. Should be interesting." He shifted the plastic bag from one hand to the other. "You know, I was talking with Chelsea last night after we got home. We both felt terrible about that awkward moment with your cousin. Family stuff is always complicated."

Ellie's face burned. "It's fine."

"If you ever need anything—I mean, if he's bothering you—I know people. Resources. Chelsea does a lot of charity work—crisis counseling at Riverside, so..."

"We're fine."

Derek nodded slowly. "You know, Ellie, Ben's lucky to have your support. With the board meeting coming up, character counts for a lot. Anything... unstable... could really tip the scales on Thursday."

The words landed like a threat wrapped in concern.

"I'll tell Ben you stopped by." She reached for the bag.

"Actually, mind if I just run these down to the workshop myself? I know where the basement entrance is. Save you the trouble of dealing with it."

Ellie hesitated. Something felt off about the request, but she couldn't articulate why. "Sure. The basement door is around back."

"I know." Derek's smile widened. "Won't take a minute."

She watched him disappear around the side of the house, the plastic bag swinging in his grip. Through the kitchen window, she tracked his progress—a blur of white tennis clothes moving past the rhododendrons, then nothing. The basement had a separate exterior entrance Ben used when hauling lumber.

Derek was gone for three minutes. Maybe four. When he reappeared, the plastic bag was gone, and he was tucking something into his pocket.

"All set," he called, waving as he climbed into the BMW. "Tell Ben I left everything on his workbench."

Ellie watched until the car disappeared around the corner, her mind working. Something Derek had said at dinner. Something that didn't add up. She couldn't quite grasp it, but it was there, nagging at her.

She returned to the kitchen, where Lily was building an elaborate tower with blocks.

The rest of the morning passed in domestic routine—laundry, cleaning, making lunch that neither of them ate much of. Ben didn't come home at noon. He texted at one o'clock:

Sorry, this is taking longer than expected. Be home by dinner. Love you.

Ellie read the message three times, looking for subtext that wasn't there.

At three o'clock, her phone buzzed with a news alert:

BREAKING: Willow Pond Police report new sighting of suspected predator near elementary school. Gray hoodie, medical mask. Witnesses urged to contact authorities.

Ellie's stomach dropped. She read the alert twice, then deleted it before Lily could see.

The afternoon dragged. Four o'clock came and went. Five. Lily wanted to watch TV, so Ellie put on a movie and sat beside her on the couch, only half-watching. Through the window, she could see the sky darkening, clouds rolling in from the west. Rain soon, probably. The weather matched her mood.

Lily laughed at something on screen, her small body curled against the armrest, completely absorbed. Ellie watched her daughter's face—innocent, trusting, safe in this moment—and felt something crack inside her chest.

She couldn't just sit here. Couldn't just wait for Ben to come home and pretend everything was normal. The questions were eating her alive, and sitting still only made them louder.

Ellie stood, touching Lily's shoulder. "I'm going to be downstairs for a minute, sweetie. Okay?"

"Uh-huh." Lily didn't look away from the screen.

She usually avoided the basement; it was Ben's domain. But her feet carried her down the stairs before she could talk herself out of it.

The workshop smelled of sawdust and machine oil, achingly familiar scents that made her chest tight. Ben's tools hung in neat rows on the pegboard. The half-finished dollhouse for Lily's birthday sat on the workbench, its tiny windows waiting for glass.

Ellie moved through the space slowly, not sure what she was looking for. Evidence of innocence? Evidence of guilt? Her hand trailed along the workbench, past the circular saw, past the jar of wood screws, past—

She stopped.

The storage cabinet in the corner stood slightly ajar. Ben was meticulous about keeping it closed; he worried about Lily getting into the power tools. Ellie pulled the door open.

On the top shelf, folded neatly beside a box of drill bits, was a gray hoodie.

Her breath caught.

Ben didn't wear hoodies. He wore button-downs, even on weekends. Sweaters in winter. His single concession to casual was the old flannel shirt by the back door.

She pulled the hoodie down with trembling hands. Cheap fabric, a no-name brand with a small logo she didn't recognize. The material felt stiff, like it had been washed once, maybe twice. Not new, but not well-worn either.

Gray hoodie. The alert in the app had said gray hoodie.

This was nothing. This was paranoia. Someone could have left it here—one of Ben's colleagues who'd borrowed the workshop, maybe. Or he'd picked it up at Goodwill for doing messy projects. There were a thousand explanations.

But why hide it in the cabinet? Why not hang it with his flannel, or toss it in the rag pile if it was for dirty work?

Her fingers found something else on the shelf: *mirrored sunglasses*, the kind that hid your eyes completely. Also unfamiliar. Ben wore Ray-Bans, tortoiseshell frames he'd had since before they were married.

The pieces shifted in her mind like a puzzle she didn't want to solve. Gray hoodie and sunglasses—a disguise? No. That was insane.

But the words from the news echoed: *The predator—a man in a gray hoodie and sunglasses—approaching children at the park.*

Ellie's hands shook as she refolded the hoodie, placed it exactly where she'd found it. The sunglasses went back too, tucked against the shelf's edge. She closed the cabinet door carefully, quietly, as if someone might hear.

She'd ask him about it—later. There was probably a simple explanation.

But the image stayed with her as she climbed back up the stairs—gray fabric, neatly folded, hidden. And those mirrored sunglasses, reflecting nothing but her own distorted face.

At five-thirty, she heard Ben's car in the driveway.

She met him at the door, and the look on his

face immediately cut through the fear that had been building since she'd found the hoodie in the basement. He looked wrecked—not just tired, but shaken. His hair was sticking up like he'd been running his hands through it, and there were coffee stains on his shirt.

"What happened?"

"Nothing. Just a long day." He pulled off his coat, hung it on the hook by the door. "Where's Lily?"

"Living room. Ben, you look—"

"I'm fine." He moved past her toward the kitchen, avoiding her eyes. "I just need some water."

She followed him, watched him fill a glass from the tap and drain it in three long swallows. His hand shook slightly as he set the glass down.

"Derek stopped by this morning," she said.

Ben's shoulders tensed. "What did he want?"

"He said he borrowed a wrench."

"A wrench." Ben laughed, a hollow sound. "Right. Where is it?"

"He said he left it on your workbench."

He nodded and leaned against the counter, staring at nothing. The kitchen light threw shadows under his eyes, made him look older than thirty-seven.

"Ben, what's going on?"

"Nothing."

"That's not true."

"Ellie, please. I don't want to talk about it right now."

"Is it the promotion? Is something wrong with the board meeting?"

"I said I don't want to talk about it." His voice had

gone sharp—not angry, exactly, but strained to the breaking point.

She stepped back. "Okay."

They looked at each other across the kitchen, and for the first time in twelve years of marriage, Ellie felt like she was looking at a stranger. This man with the hollow eyes and the coffee-stained shirt and the secrets he wouldn't share—who was he?

"I'm going to take a shower," Ben said. "Can you handle dinner?"

"Sure."

He left without kissing her. She heard his footsteps on the stairs, heard the bathroom door close, heard the water start running. In the living room, Lily was singing along with her movie, her voice high and pure and heartbreakingly innocent.

Ellie stood alone in the kitchen and felt the first real tendril of fear wind its way around her heart.

Something was wrong. Something was deeply, fundamentally wrong.

And whatever it was, Ben wasn't telling her.

* * *

That night, after Lily was in bed, after the dishes were done, after Ben had disappeared into his workshop in the basement "to work on Lily's birthday present," Ellie found herself standing in the kitchen with her phone in her hand.

She pulled up the local news site. The sketch was there—an artist's rendering based on witness descriptions of the Heron Marsh predator: a man in a gray hoodie, medical mask pulled up over his nose and mouth, mirrored sunglasses obscuring his eyes. The caption read: Subject described as approximately 6 feet tall, slim, age 30-40. If you have any information, please contact the Willow Pond Police Department.

Ellie looked toward the basement door. She could hear the saw whining below, a jagged sound that vibrated in the floorboards.

On the counter, the police sketch stared up at her. The artist had drawn a man without a face, just a mask and sunglasses and a gray hoodie. A generic boogeyman.

She looked at the coat rack by the back door. The hook where Ben's old, worn blue-plaid flannel shirt always hung—the one he'd purchased well before they'd even gotten together, faded and soft from years of wear—was empty.

No. The word was a physical jolt.

She'd never seen a hoodie in this house. Ben didn't own hoodies. He never had. It wasn't his style—he'd made that clear years ago, some comment about looking like he was trying too hard to be younger than he was.

She forced herself to look away, to focus on the dirty dishes, the mundane reality of their life. Ben was building a dollhouse. He was a father. He was her husband.

But the saw stopped. Silence rushed back into the kitchen, heavier than before. Footsteps crunched across the concrete floor—heavy, deliberate steps that matched the cadence she'd heard last night.

The basement door opened.

Ben stood there, wiping his hands on a rag. He was wearing his blue-plaid flannel buttoned over his t-shirt, sawdust clinging to his shoulders like snow. In the harsh kitchen light, with the shadows cutting across his face, he didn't look like the sketch on the counter. But how would he look in a grey hoodie?

"Hey," he said. His eyes flicked to the sketch on her phone, then up to hers. The air in the kitchen grew instantly thin. "You okay?"

"Fine." Her voice sounded brittle. "Just tired."

"You should go to bed. I'll lock up down here."

He reached for the deadbolt on the basement door—the key flashing silver in his hand. The key she didn't have.

"Ben?"

He paused, hand on the lock. "Yeah?"

"Wednesday night." The question clawed its way up her throat. "The meeting. What time did it actually end?"

Ben's jaw tightened. "I don't know. Six-thirty, maybe? Why?"

"And you came straight home after?"

"Ellie, what is this about?"

"Nothing. I'm just asking."

"No, you're not just asking. You're interrogating me." He moved closer, and she saw genuine hurt in his face. "Do you not trust me? Is that what this is?"

"Of course I trust you—"

"Then why are you asking me for an alibi?"

The word hung between them. She hadn't said it, but he had, and now it was out there, impossible to take back.

"I'm sorry," she said. "I'm just stressed. With

everything going on—the park, and Will showing up, and this board meeting—I'm not sleeping well."

Ben's expression softened. He reached for her, pulled her into his arms, and she let herself lean against his chest, breathing in sawdust and laundry detergent and the familiar scent of him.

"I know you're scared," he said into her hair. "I'm scared too. But we're okay. All three of us. We're going to be okay."

She wanted to believe him. God, she wanted to believe him.

But when she closed her eyes, all she could see was that sketch in the news—the anonymous man in the gray hoodie, the monster who could be anyone.

Or everyone.

Or the one person she'd promised to love and trust for the rest of her life.

CHAPTER 4

Sunday morning

Ellie hadn't slept. She'd tried—gone to bed around midnight, stared at the ceiling for three hours, finally given up around 3:00 AM and come downstairs. Now she sat at the kitchen table, watching dawn creep across the backyard, the hoodie from Ben's workshop consuming her thoughts.

She should have asked him about it last night. Should have demanded an explanation. Instead, she'd frozen, terrified of what his answer might be.

The sound of the garage door opening made her jump. Ben's car.

He'd left at 5:30 AM—she'd heard the alarm, heard him moving quietly through the dark house, trying not to wake anyone. "Early meeting," he'd mumbled when she'd asked. "The preliminary board review—the chairman is visiting England. I'll be back by eight."

He came through the door now looking worse than when he'd left. His shirt was wrinkled, his tie loosened, dark circles carved under his eyes.

"How did it go?" Ellie forced the words past the tightness in her throat.

"Long." He dropped his briefcase by the door, rubbed both hands over his face. "You know how it is—everyone loves to hear themselves talk. But they want me to present at Thursday's board meeting. That's got to be a good sign, right? They want me, El. Finally. It's all happening."

"That's wonderful," she said, but her voice came out flat.

She wanted to be happy for him. Wanted to celebrate. But all she could see was that gray hoodie, those mirrored sunglasses, hidden in his workshop like secrets.

He moved to embrace her, but she stiffened without meaning to.

"What's wrong?" He studied her face. "Did something happen?"

Yes, she wanted to say. I found evidence in your workshop that you might be the Heron Marsh Predator. Tell me I'm wrong. Please, tell me I'm wrong.

"Nothing," she said. "Just tired."

A few hours later, the doorbell shattered the tense silence.

Ben had gone upstairs to shower. Ellie was loading the dishwasher, moving on autopilot, when the sharp ring froze her mid-motion.

Through the front window, she could see two uniformed policemen standing on the porch. Her heart plummeted.

Even before she opened the door, she knew.

"Benjamin Carlson?" The older one held up a badge. "We need you to come with us for questioning."

Ellie gripped the doorframe. "Questioning? For what?"

"Ma'am, if you could get your husband—"

"I'm here." Ben appeared at the top of the stairs, his hair still damp from the shower. His face had gone pale. "What's this about?"

"We need you to come to the station to answer some questions regarding the Heron Marsh incidents."

"The—" Ben's voice caught. "You think I'm—"

"We're not accusing you of anything, Mr. Carlson. We just need to ask some questions."

Ellie watched Ben descend the stairs, watched him reach for her hand. His fingers were ice cold.

"This is a mistake," she said. "My husband hasn't done anything wrong."

"We apologize for the inconvenience, ma'am," the older policeman said. "If your husband is innocent, he has nothing to worry about. Right, Mr. Carlson? If you can account for your whereabouts at the relevant times, this will all be cleared up quickly."

Ben's grip on Ellie's hand tightened. "I need to get dressed. And I want to call my lawyer."

"Of course. We'll wait."

When Ben went upstairs to change, one policeman stayed in the living room while the other stepped outside.

Ellie followed Ben up the stairs. "What's happening?"

"I don't know." His hands shook as he pulled on a clean shirt. "Someone must have—I don't understand how—"

"We'll fix this," Ellie said, even as doubt clawed at her throat.

Ten minutes later, she watched through the front window as they led Ben to an unmarked car. He looked back at her once, his face a mask of fear and confusion.

Then he was gone.

Lily appeared at the top of the stairs, Mr. Pemberton

tucked under her arm, just as the car disappeared around the corner.

"Mommy? Where did Daddy go?"

Ellie forced herself to smile. "Just to talk to some people about work, honey. He'll be back soon."

"Is Daddy getting moved now?" Lily asked, rubbing her eyes. "To the new job?"

Ellie knelt down to Lily's level. "Maybe, sweetheart. We'll have to wait and see."

She couldn't tell her daughter the truth. Not yet. Not until she understood what was happening herself.

"Why don't we call Grandma?" Ellie said, keeping her voice light. "Maybe you can spend the day with her."

Lily's face brightened. "Can I?"

"Let me call her right now."

When her mother answered, she immediately sensed something was wrong.

"Of course I'll take Lily for a few days," she said, concerned. "But what's going on? You and Ben haven't had a fight, have you?"

"No, no—please don't ask more right now. I'll explain everything later."

The prospect of days at Grandma's house—with favorite meals, ice cream, and constant baking—made Lily dizzy with excitement. She rushed to gather Mr. Pemberton and other essential toys into a big pile. Once everything was packed, Grace arrived and took her.

An hour later, she still hadn't heard from Ben. The phone had beeped once—Grace phoning to confirm Lily's settling in just fine.

"But what is this Lily's saying?" Grace asked, voice

rising. "That Ben was picked up by two men? That sounds strange—"

Ellie forced a laugh and threw together an explanation about colleagues picking him up for a meeting.

When the phone finally rang, relief flooded through her. Ellie grabbed it.

"Hello!" she answered breathlessly, waiting for Ben's calm voice.

But it was Derek.

"Hey, Ellie. What's up with Ben? Is he sick?"

"Sick? Yes, yes—he's not feeling well."

"You sound strange. What's really wrong with him?"

Stammering, Ellie repeated her explanation while wondering if someone from the company had witnessed the pickup. Probably not Derek and Chelsea. But hadn't they hired a new office assistant who lived in the neighborhood?

She felt drained when the call ended. This was just a preview of what was coming. And she hated lying more than anything. Now she was forced to...

Forced? What was forcing her? Why didn't she just tell the truth? Did she have doubts deep down?

She stood staring at the phone for several minutes. These interviews could take hours, she'd heard. The suspect would be worn down, trapped...

Though the car was in the garage, she called a taxi instead. She felt too shaken to drive.

The taxi arrived. Ellie huddled in the corner and pulled out her phone, unable to sit still. A news alert glowed on the screen:

BREAKING: ARREST MADE IN HERON

MARSH CASE. TIPSTER LEADS POLICE TO LOCAL MAN.

Her first reaction was relief, but then she went cold. They meant Ben.

Marcus lit up with a welcoming smile when he opened the door and saw who'd rung the bell. But his expression quickly turned serious when he noticed Ellie's tear-stained face.

"What's wrong?" he asked, putting his arm around her shoulders and leading her into the large living room, where she sank onto one of the deep sofas near the fireplace.

"Drink this and tell me what happened."

He poured a generous glass of brandy and sat beside her.

Through halting words and several crying jags, Ellie finally got the whole story out. Marcus looked shaken. At first he seemed calm, but as the details accumulated, shocked dismay crossed his face.

"It's not possible," he said. "I refuse to believe it. I've known Ben for years—longer than you have, Ellie— and I have to say it's completely unthinkable. You said they kept him?"

Ellie nodded.

"Well, it's just an interview. Any minute now they'll release him and—"

She shook her head and told him about the news alert.

"I have a friend on the force," Marcus said thoughtfully. "I'll call him."

He went to his study and returned shortly.

"He promised to find out what's going on," he said, his gaze drifting to the window, not meeting her eyes. "He'll call when he knows something."

Fifteen minutes passed, during which Marcus made earnest but failed attempts to distract her. Finally, the phone rang. The call was brief, and Ellie could see immediately that the news wasn't good.

"It was hard for him to find out much," Marcus said evasively. "You know, he works in a different department—"

"Don't dodge. Tell me the truth," Ellie said sharply.

"Well, it looks bad for Ben," Marcus admitted. "There's going to be a bail hearing soon."

Ellie broke down. Sobbing like a child, she buried her face in a cushion.

"Calm down," Marcus urged. "For your own sake, you need to pull yourself together—and for Ben's sake."

She cried inconsolably, but then she suddenly stopped and jumped up from the sofa.

The hoodie! It was still in the workshop!

Only now did she tell Marcus about what she'd found.

"I should have gotten rid of it," she said anxiously. "If the police find it—"

"That's strange," Marcus said. "You don't think Lily could have put it there? Kids love to dress up. Maybe she hid it so she could keep it."

Ellie dismissed the idea.

"Lily doesn't even go into the workshop. Ben always keeps it locked."

"The basement window?" he suggested.

The thought hadn't occurred to Ellie.

Before leaving, Ellie called the police station and asked to speak with Detective Reyes.

"Mrs. Carlson." His tone was carefully neutral. "What can I do for you?"

"Derek Thornton," she said. "Ben's coworker. He came by yesterday and mentioned the hoodie you found. He said, 'some hoodie in a basement.' But that wasn't public information. How would he know where you found it?"

A pause. "Are you sure he said that?"

"Positive. He knew what you found and where you found it."

"That's... interesting." She heard papers rustling. "We'll look into it. Thank you for calling."

After she hung up, Marcus arrived. "Ready?"

She nodded, but her mind was still on Derek's slip.

* * *

Marcus offered to drive her home so they could check. As he helped her on with her coat, she found herself in his arms without either of them quite knowing how it happened.

"They took him, Marcus. They think he did it."

"Ellie!" he said angrily. "Don't even think that way. Ben isn't some twisted person who goes after little girls—you should know that. Now pull yourself together. I'm absolutely convinced it won't be long before he's cleared."

He led her out to his car and drove off. Ellie sat rigid, staring at nothing. Only when they passed Heron Marsh did her gaze pull inevitably toward the park.

Someone out there is guilty, she thought. Somewhere there's some poor wretch with a bad conscience. Or maybe he's so damaged he doesn't even understand what he's done. It could be anyone: the man waiting at that bus stop, or the painter at that construction site, or the mailman.

Suddenly a comforting thought struck her. If the predator committed another assault—and didn't they always?—then Ben would be released and finally cleared of suspicion. She almost wished it would happen.

The small basement window faced the backyard. Ellie and Marcus went straight there, and Marcus knelt to examine it. He gripped the frame and tried to pry it open, but the window wouldn't budge. The paint had sealed it shut.

"It hasn't been opened since Ben painted these frames last summer," he said, standing and wiping his hands on his trousers.

The fragile hope collapsed, and Ellie leaned heavily against the wall. Marcus put his arm around her shoulders and gently guided her toward the front entrance. When they rounded the corner, they stopped at the sight of two men who had just gotten out of a car and were walking up the path. Marcus's arm dropped.

"Mrs. Carlson?" one of the men said. "My name is Detective Reyes. You understand why we're here, I think. We have authorization to search your home— yes, your husband was smart enough to sign the consent form himself. Here, you can see it. So if you'll let us in—"

"You mean you're going to—to search—"

　　　　　　　　　　　　　　　　　　

"We're going to take a look around, yes."

Ellie mechanically inserted the key in the lock and pushed open the door. Reyes stepped inside without waiting for an invitation, but Marcus rushed forward with an angry protest about this invasion of private property. He was silenced when the paper signed by Ben was thrust into his hand.

"Does this gentleman live here?" Reyes asked, looking from Marcus to Ellie, an eyebrow raised.

"No—he's a good friend who—"

"Is that so? A good friend, you say?"

"While I don't have the authority to throw out your good friend, Mrs. Carlson, we'd prefer it if he left."

Marcus decided it was wisest to follow the suggestion, but first he pulled Ellie into an embrace.

"I'll be back," he promised. "You can always count on me."

After Marcus left, Ellie stood in the empty hallway, her mind racing. The police were here. They were going to search everything. And suddenly she needed to know—needed to see for herself what was in Ben's workshop.

The detectives behaved as correctly and considerately as circumstances allowed, but Ellie felt sick watching them rifle through her and Ben's private belongings.

"We're just doing our job," they said apologetically.

At one point, Reyes took Ellie aside and asked a series of extremely personal questions. He didn't even hesitate to imply what Marcus's presence had suggested to him. Ellie tried to stay composed and answer calmly so as not to betray her distress.

While Reyes questioned Ellie, his colleague went through the basement. He'd slipped away quietly without her noticing, but his footsteps coming back up were heavy and deliberate. Ellie's heart nearly stopped when she saw what he'd found.

Reyes held up a clear plastic bag. Inside, gray fabric was bunched against a pair of mirrored sunglasses. He looked straight at Ellie.

"Mrs. Carlson," he said. "Do these belong to your husband?"

CHAPTER 5

The detectives' footsteps faded down the driveway. A car door slammed, the engine turned over, and the heavy silence of the house rushed back in to fill the space.

Ellie gripped the doorframe, her knuckles white. They had the hoodie. They had the sunglasses.

Thank God Lily isn't here. The thought made her nauseous. Strangers tearing through a five-year-old's bedroom, lifting her mattress, touching her things— Ellie pressed a hand to her mouth.

"Ben," she whispered into thin air. "Tell me it's not true."

The workshop. The hoodie.

She'd meant to ask Ben about it—meant to go down there and look again, make sure she hadn't imagined it. But everything had happened so fast—the police arriving, Ben being taken away.

Now it was too late. And there was no innocent explanation—

She couldn't finish the thought.

The front gate clicked. Ellie flinched, wiping her face with her sleeve. Through the blur of moisture, she saw Marcus striding up the walk. He didn't look at the police cars retreating down the street; his eyes were locked on her.

"I waited just down the road," he said, stepping inside and closing the door firmly behind him. "Did they find anything?"

Ellie stared at the floor. "They went to the workshop."

"And?"

"They found the hoodie. And the glasses."

Marcus let out a breath, running a hand through his hair. "I don't understand. Could it have been your cousin? You said Will was here Friday."

"Will barely makes it past the front hall." Ellie moved to the kitchen, needing something to do with her hands. She filled the kettle, though she didn't want tea. "He and Ben can't stand each other. Besides, Will stands out. If he was walking around Heron Marsh, someone would have called the cops on him for vagrancy, not assault."

Marcus nodded, his brow creased with worry.

It helped to have him here, Ellie thought. Otherwise the waiting would be unbearable. Her eyes kept drifting to her phone on the kitchen counter. Why hadn't Ben called? Maybe he had an explanation for the hoodie—something reasonable that would clear everything up in an instant.

Then doubt crashed over her again. It wasn't just the hoodie. Someone had reported him. Someone had given the police his name. That meant there had to be other evidence.

After an hour of anxious silence, Ellie convinced Marcus to call his contact on the force again. The news wasn't good.

"Ben's still being questioned," Marcus relayed the sparse information he'd been given. "But who knows—maybe the real predator will strike again and get caught."

"The real one," Ellie said.

"The real one," she repeated, and something hardened in her voice. "Do you think they'll let me see him?"

"Not right now. But his lawyer's on the way. You should talk to him."

* * *

The lawyer didn't come in person. He sent one of his associates instead—a young man who had recently finished his legal training. When Ellie answered the door, David Ashford introduced himself with a perfunctory handshake, already glancing past her into the house.

She showed him into the living room, aware of Marcus lingering in the kitchen doorway. Their eyes met briefly, and Marcus gave a small nod before retreating, pulling the kitchen door partially closed to give them privacy. She heard the quiet clink of dishes as he busied himself, staying out of the way.

David Ashford made a poor impression on Ellie. He settled onto the couch with his briefcase, checking his phone before finally looking up at her. He seemed casual, superior, and uninterested in the case—like this was just another routine appointment in a busy day.

It surprised her that Ben hadn't insisted on their regular attorney, but she took it as a sign that he didn't think it was necessary, that his conscience was clear.

"Your husband is going to be formally detained," young Ashford said, settling uninvited into the most comfortable chair in the living room. "The charges against him are serious, obviously. But we'll see, Mrs. Carlson—maybe it won't turn out so badly after all."

As if it isn't already bad enough, Ellie thought

bitterly. Ben had been taken away by police, suspected of a terrible crime. The mere fact that he'd been accused would poison their lives for years. It would damage him at work, no question.

While Ellie forced herself to hide her distaste, she answered a long series of questions that seemed irrelevant to her. When she coolly said goodbye to David Ashford, she knew she wasn't going to get any help from him.

But the visit had brought something good—a new determination had taken hold of her. If this was going to end well, it depended on her.

"So?" Marcus said when Ellie returned to the kitchen. He was leaning against the counter with a mug of coffee in his hands—he'd clearly helped himself while she was occupied. "I can tell by your face you got good news!"

"No, Marcus. But I've started to understand that something's wrong here. Nothing can stop me now. I'm going to do whatever it takes to clear Ben's name."

Marcus took both her hands in his. "That's what I want to hear!"

He gave her hands an extra squeeze before releasing them.

"How are you planning to proceed?" he asked. "Can I help somehow?"

Ellie explained that her first step was to bring Lily home. She'd been told that Ben's name wouldn't be released to the media—but what did that matter? By evening, everyone in the neighborhood would know he'd been detained. People could think what they wanted, but they wouldn't be able to accuse her of cowardice.

Marcus offered to pick up Lily after Ellie had called her mother and explained what had happened. Grace became hysterical, crying and carrying on, unable to understand how Ellie could be so calm about it.

Ellie's fighting spirit grew.

After Marcus left, she opened her laptop and began searching for everything she could find about the Heron Marsh Predator. She hoped to find something that would prove Ben couldn't have committed the assaults. The articles were vague about timing, however, and only in one case were specific times mentioned—in connection with the most serious assault. A seven-year-old girl had been grabbed near the playground the previous Wednesday between six and seven in the evening. She'd managed to break free and run to safety, but the incident had escalated the investigation.

Wednesday, Ellie remembered. I was getting my hair cut. Ben had a long meeting and didn't get home until seven-thirty. She recalled it clearly because she'd rushed straight home from the salon to get the meatloaf ready, but it had dried out in the oven anyway.

There was his alibi! Derek had been at the same meeting. They must have been on their way home when the murder took place.

Marcus returned with Lily. The girl had understood little of what was happening and was delighted to have first visited Grandma and then been picked up by Marcus, who was her absolute favorite. Her happiness increased when she learned Marcus would stay with her while Ellie visited Derek and Chelsea.

"Then you have to play piano," Lily decided. "First we'll do 'Twinkle Twinkle,' then 'You Are My Sunshine,' then 'The Wheels on the Bus'..."

Marcus smiled and followed willingly when Lily dragged him toward the piano in the living room. The last thing Ellie heard was Lily singing children's songs at full volume to Marcus's accompaniment.

Thank God for friends, she thought. Derek and Chelsea will surely help out when they hear how bad things are for Ben.

* * *

Chelsea opened the door, and Ellie immediately understood she already knew something.

"Come in, you poor thing," she said. "What a terrible situation! Derek just mentioned we should stop by, but I didn't want to intrude."

Ellie stood stunned. How on earth had they found out what happened? But before she could ask, Derek came hurrying over and pressed her hand, solemn and grave as if offering condolences at a funeral.

"Now just take it easy," he said in a fatherly tone, helping her with her coat. "We were just having a drink to calm our nerves."

"But I don't understand—" Ellie began, looking from one to the other. "How do you know...?"

Derek looked uncomfortable and studied the floor.

A long, painful silence followed. Finally, Derek felt compelled to continue.

"Word gets around, you know. The receptionist at work lives with a guy who's a journalist..."

Ellie silently accepted the drink Derek handed her. Yes, she knew how "word got around." Other people's misfortunes were the best entertainment. And Derek had done little to stop the talk.

Ben's absence serves Derek's interests, she thought suddenly. Even if Ben is cleared of all suspicion, this could tip the scales in Derek's favor.

She felt ashamed of the thought. Derek and Chelsea had been good friends. It wasn't fair to suspect him of trying to benefit from the situation.

"I was hoping you could help me, Derek," Ellie said, and couldn't help the note of uncertainty in her voice.

Derek jumped up, placed both hands on her shoulders, and looked deep into her eyes.

"Of course, Ellie," he assured her. "Of course! We were just talking about it before you came, weren't we, Chelsea?"

Chelsea nodded silently.

"Ben needs an alibi," Ellie continued. "You had a meeting with representatives from a German company the day that terrible attack happened. You were there too, right?"

"Last Wednesday, wasn't it? That's right."

"Ben wasn't home until seven-thirty. You must have been on your way home when it happened?"

Derek wrinkled his forehead, straining to remember clearly.

"Let's see. Yes, we had guests coming over—I was

worried I wouldn't make it in time. But I was home by five at the latest."

"By five?" Ellie felt the blood rush to her head. Instead of providing Ben with an alibi, she'd achieved the opposite.

"Yes," Derek confirmed. "We drove in my car—we had a meeting with the Germans at their hotel first, then I dropped him off at the company afterward. I remember that clearly."

Ellie didn't stay long after that news. Not just because her hopes for an alibi had been dashed, but because she understood Ben had hidden something from her. What had he been doing after he and Derek parted ways?

Grim and discouraged, she came home to find the living room lights on. Were they still at the piano? Ellie sighed. Poor Marcus—she was taking advantage of him. And Lily could be stubborn.

She stepped inside and found everything quiet. No piano music. No singing. Confused, she went upstairs. The door to Lily's room stood wide open, and inside, Lily lay sleeping peacefully. On a chair by the bed sat Marcus with his chin against his chest. Ellie had to smile—he'd fallen asleep over "Goodnight Moon."

* * *

On Monday morning, the headlines screaming from her phone were bad, but the looks from the other parents at preschool were even worse. Ellie turned around outside the school and called her mother to watch Lily instead. By the time she turned the corner to her street, she felt flayed alive.

A figure sat on her front steps.

Marcus. Relief washed through her. She quickened her pace. Marcus would know how to handle the lawyer. Marcus would tell her what to do.

But as she got closer, the figure shifted. It wasn't Marcus's broad shoulders. It was a slouch. A shabby coat.

Will.

He looked worse than usual—pale, puffy-faced, shivering in the mild afternoon air.

"Got anything to eat, Ellie?" He didn't stand up. "I'm broke."

"I don't have cash, Will."

"I didn't ask for cash. I asked for food."

Against her better judgment, she unlocked the door. She couldn't leave him on the porch for the neighbors to stare at. "Five minutes. You eat, then you go."

Inside, Will devoured a ham sandwich with shaking hands. The bravado he usually carried—the big business ideas, the investments—was gone. He looked like a frightened animal.

"So," he said, wiping mayonnaise from his lip. "The lawyer was here earlier. Saw his fancy car."

Ellie froze. "You were watching the house?"

"I was waiting for you. Heard him talking on his way out. Loud guy. Said something about witnesses?" Will's eyes narrowed, a spark of the old cunning returning. "Two witnesses who saw Ben in the glasses?"

"That's none of your business."

"It is if I'm family to a predator." Will leaned back, picking his teeth. "Police are going to be looking for character witnesses, right? People to say whether Ben had a... temper."

The air in the kitchen grew cold. "Get out, Will."

"I'm just saying. Testimony is flexible. Memory is a tricky thing." He tapped his temple. "For five thousand, I could remember Ben being a saint. For free... well, I might remember that time he kicked my dog."

"You never had a dog."

"See? Details." He smirked. "Police believe the worst, Ellie. And right now, Ben looks like the worst."

"Extortion, then."

"I've been through worse," he said.

At that moment, a car stopped outside the gate. A flicker of uncertainty crossed Will's face, but Ellie felt relieved. It was Marcus arriving—thank God she didn't have to be alone with Will any longer.

"I'm sorry I'm late, but I had some things to take care of and— Oh, excuse me, I thought you were alone."

Marcus looked questioningly from one to the other.

"It's just my cousin you've probably heard about," Ellie said. "He was just leaving."

Will had a retort on his tongue but swallowed it. Marcus was tall and solid, and Will didn't take obvious risks.

"Think over my proposal," he said, straightening up.

Marcus caught the tense atmosphere in an instant and took a step toward Will.

"Has he been bothering you?" he asked. "Should I help him on his way?"

"Will's leaving on his own. Right, Will?"

"That's right," he said, slipping past them. "And you know where to find me!"

"What on earth did he mean by that?" Marcus wondered, glancing after Will, who was nearly running toward the gate.

Ellie burst into tears. Between sobs, she told him what had happened.

"Empty threat, nothing more," Marcus said. "Could it have been him who made the anonymous tip against Ben?"

"Impossible. He didn't know anything until Ashford came and— Oh right! I'm supposed to visit Ben! I'd better hurry if I'm going to make it before picking up Lily from Mom."

Marcus drove her. What would she have done without Marcus?

And it wasn't until she sat in the car that it truly hit her what was about to happen. The thought of seeing Ben after all the terrible things that had occurred made her tremble. How had Ben taken it? How would she react? Did he still see the situation as optimistically as he had the morning he was taken away?

Chapter 6

Monday afternoon

The police station was a flat-roofed brick block at the edge of downtown. It looked less like a place of law and more like a utility substation—windowless and grimy. Marcus found a parking spot under a row of maples, their leaves already curling brown at the edges.

"I can't do this," Ellie said, her hand frozen on the door handle.

Marcus turned to her. "You have to. You know you have to." His voice was firm. "I'll be right behind you."

Ellie unclicked her seatbelt.

Inside, fluorescent lights hummed overhead, casting a greenish pall over everything. A woman behind bulletproof glass slid forms across the counter without looking up. Ellie signed where indicated, printed her name, dated each document. Her hand shook so hard the signature didn't look like hers.

"Through that door. Third room on the left."

The hallway smelled of industrial cleaner and stale coffee. Ellie's flats squeaked against the linoleum. Marcus walked beside her, his hand hovering near the small of her back but not quite touching.

At the door, Detective Reyes appeared. "Mrs. Carlson. You'll have twenty minutes."

"Can I—" Marcus began.

"Just family." The detective held up a large hand.

Ellie nodded. Marcus squeezed her shoulder and stepped back.

The room was bare except for a metal table and two chairs bolted to the floor. A camera blinked red in the corner. Ellie sat and folded her hands on the table's cold surface. Her wedding ring clicked against the metal.

The door opened.

Ben stood in the threshold, an officer at his elbow. His hair stuck up on one side. The orange jumpsuit hung loose on his frame—he'd lost weight, somehow, in just two days. Dark circles carved crescents beneath his eyes, and his jaw was rough with stubble. But his face scared her the most. It wasn't fear she saw there. It was resignation. He looked like a man who had already stopped waiting for the end.

"Benjamin," she whispered, using his full name without meaning to.

He shuffled to the chair across from her. The officer retreated but remained by the door.

Ellie reached across the table. Ben stared at her hand for a long moment before taking it. His fingers were cold.

"You know I believe you," she said. The words tumbled out. "You didn't do this. You couldn't. Not ever. Not—"

"Ellie." His voice rasped, unused. "Don't."

"Don't what?"

"Don't make promises. Don't—" He pulled his hand back, pressed both palms against his forehead. "I don't know how to do this."

"Look at me."

He didn't.

"Ben. Look at me."

When he finally lifted his head, his eyes were wet. "I'm sorry."

The words landed like stones in her chest. "For what?"

"For all of it. For—" He gestured vaguely, encompassing the room, the situation, everything. "For being so shut down when you got here. For not fighting harder. For letting this happen."

"You didn't let anything happen. Someone did this to you. Someone planted—"

"I know." He leaned back, the chair scraping. "I know. But that doesn't change where I am right now."

Ellie swallowed. "Lily thinks you're on a business trip."

His face crumpled. For a moment she thought he might break, but he gathered himself, knuckled his eyes. "She asked about me?"

"Every five minutes. She wants to know if you'll bring her a present."

"God." The word came out strangled.

"She's fine. She's with Mom. She's safe and she's fine and she misses you and none of this is your fault."

They sat in silence. The clock ticked. Somewhere down the hall, a phone rang and rang.

"The lawyer," Ellie started. "The young one they sent, he's useless. I don't trust him. We need someone better."

"We can't afford better."

"Marcus said—"

"I'm not taking money from Marcus."

"Ben—"

"No." His voice hardened. "I won't be in debt to him. Not now. Not like this."

Ellie nearly laughed at the absurdity. "He's trying to help."

"I know what he's trying to do."

"What's that supposed to mean?"

Ben looked away. "Forget it."

"We're not doing this. We're not pretending everything's fine when it's not."

"I thought you wanted to believe in me."

"I do," she said.

"Then believe me when I say I'm handling the lawyer situation."

"How? From in here?"

He flinched. The officer by the door shifted his weight.

Ellie pressed her fingers to her temples.

Ben stared at her, his eyes drifting past her shoulder. "I should have fixed the lock on the back gate."

"Ben, that doesn't matter."

"I meant to do it weeks ago. If I had—"

"Focus, Ben. The lawyer."

He shook his head. "Nothing."

"Ben—"

"Time's up." The officer stepped forward.

"Wait." Ellie stood. "I need to ask you something."

Ben rose, swaying slightly. Exhaustion painted his face.

"The hoodie. The sunglasses. I found them before—" She lowered her voice. "Before they came. They were in the workshop."

"I know."

"You know?" Ellie stared at him.

"They told me. Showed me photos of what they recovered."

"But you didn't put them there. You don't own a gray hoodie."

"No."

"Then how—"

"Mrs. Carlson." The officer touched her elbow. "We need to wrap this up."

"Someone's setting you up," Ellie said. "Someone who had access to the house. Who knows where you work, what you're competing for—"

"Ellie, stop." Ben's voice went flat again. "Just—take care of Lily. That's what matters."

"You matter."

"Not right now, I don't."

The officer began steering Ben toward the door.

"I love you," Ellie called after him. "I love you, and I'm going to fix this."

He paused in the doorway, his back to her. "Forgive me," he said.

Then he was gone.

Ellie stood frozen. The words echoed. Forgive me.

The officer returned. "Ma'am, you'll need to leave."

She moved on numb legs back through the corridor, past the humming lights and antiseptic smell. Marcus waited in the lobby, scrolling through his phone. When he saw her face, he pocketed it.

"That bad?"

"I don't know what that was."

Outside, the October air felt sharp after the recycled atmosphere of the station. Ellie gulped it down, trying to clear her head.

"What did he say?" Marcus asked.

"He said—" She paused on the sidewalk. "He asked me to forgive him."

Marcus frowned. "For what?"

"That's what I'm wondering."

"Ellie."

She turned to face him. "You don't think—"

"No. Absolutely not. There's no part of me that thinks Ben did this."

"Then why would he—"

"Shame, maybe. For being accused. For putting you through this." Marcus guided her toward the car. "Or maybe he just needed to say something, and that's what came out. People break under pressure."

They climbed into the car. Marcus started the engine but didn't put it in gear.

"Where to?"

"I need to pick up Lily."

"Ellie, are you sure you should—"

"I need to see my daughter, Marcus." Her voice cracked. "I need to hold her and remember what normal feels like for five minutes. Can you understand that?"

"Of course." He pulled out of the parking lot. "Grace's place?"

"Yeah."

They drove in silence through streets Ellie had known her whole life, now made strange by everything that had happened. The coffee shop where she used to meet other moms. The pharmacy where she picked up Lily's antibiotics when she'd had that ear infection. The dry cleaner that always over-starched Ben's shirts.

Her phone buzzed. Unknown number. She declined the call.

It rang again immediately.

"Maybe you should answer," Marcus said.

Ellie lifted the phone. "Hello?"

Static crackled. Then: "Mrs. Carlson? This is David Ashford, from your husband's legal team."

The young lawyer. His voice carried that same breezy confidence she'd found so infuriating before.

"What do you want?"

"Just wanted to touch base. Update you on the arraignment schedule. Your husband will be formally charged Friday morning. We'll enter a plea of not guilty, request bail—"

"Will he get it?"

A pause. "That's hard to say. Given the nature of the charges—"

"Will he get it?"

"Probably not."

Ellie closed her eyes. "What else?"

"We're seeing some movement from the DA," Ashford said.

"What kind of movement?"

"They had a witness come forward. Someone who thought they saw Ben near the playground last Tuesday."

Ellie's breath caught. "Thought?"

"She recanted this morning. Said she wasn't sure after all—the man was wearing sunglasses and a mask, could have been anyone. Without a positive ID, the testimony's worthless."

Relief flooded through her. "So that's good news?"

"It means they're grasping at straws, Mrs. Carlson. But they still have the physical evidence from your home."

"I—" Ellie's throat closed. Could she? She'd been home with Lily. She hadn't called Ben. Hadn't texted. Had no proof of where he'd been except his word.

"Mrs. Carlson?"

"Is there anything else?"

"Not at the moment. We'll be in touch before the arraignment. And Mrs. Carlson? It might be wise to limit your contact with the press. I understand Channel 5 has been calling."

"I haven't talked to anyone."

"Good. Keep it that way."

He hung up.

Ellie lowered the phone to her lap. Marcus glanced over. "What did he say?"

"Someone identified Ben. Says she saw him at the park."

"When?"

"Last Tuesday. Four in the afternoon."

Marcus's jaw tightened. "He was at work Tuesday."

"Can we prove that?"

"His key card, security logs, office cameras—yes. We can prove it."

"Then why didn't the lawyer mention that?" Ellie felt exhausted.

"Because he's twenty-eight years old and playing at

criminal defense." Marcus took the next turn harder than necessary. "First thing tomorrow, we're finding you a real attorney."

"Ben won't take money from you."

"Then we'll find another way. What about your mother?"

"She barely has enough for herself."

"Savings? Credit cards?"

"Maxed out. We put everything into the house." Ellie stared out the window at the passing trees, their leaves beginning to turn. "We have nothing, Marcus. We're completely exposed."

They pulled up outside Grace's condo complex. Through the first-floor window, Ellie could see her mother moving around the kitchen.

"Wait here," Marcus said. "I'll get Lily."

"No. I need to—"

"Your mother's going to have questions. Let me run interference. You compose yourself."

"Marcus." Ellie's voice was steady. "I have to do this. I have to talk to her."

Grace was waiting in the hallway before Ellie had even knocked on the door.

"Is that you, Ellie?"

"Who else would it be?"

Grace opened the door and crossed her arms. "Where have you been? You said you'd pick up Lily hours ago. When you didn't answer your phone, I started calling around—your friends said they hadn't seen you since yesterday. Said you ran out looking upset."

Ellie's eyebrows drew together. What right did her

mother have, calling around, checking up on her like she was a teenager? Wasn't she an adult with her own family?

But when she saw the fear in her mother's eyes, Ellie understood the root of her panic and pulled her into a hug.

"I would never do that. I have too much to live for. Lily and Ben... and you."

Grace wiped a tear from the corner of her eye.

"I was so worried," she said. "After you left the station yesterday without a word, and then you were gone all afternoon today—I didn't know what to think. That Derek has called here several times asking if you'd made it back yet."

Ellie hid a bitter smile.

"I'm glad you have such good friends," Grace said with a silent sigh as Lily appeared in the hallway. Ellie scooped her up, swung her around.

"Mommy!" Lily squirmed in her arms. "Guess what! Grandma let me make cookies and I put way too many chocolate chips in, but they still tasted good and—" She paused, studying Ellie's face. "Mommy, why do you look sad?"

"I'm not sad, baby. I'm happy to see you."

"Is Daddy still on his trip?"

The lie stuck in Ellie's throat. "Yes."

"When's he coming home?"

"Soon. I hope soon."

Ellie held Lily's hand as they walked to where Marcus waited by the car. Behind them, Grace appeared in the doorway, waving tentatively. Ellie waved back but kept moving forward, couldn't face her mother's worry, her questions, her barely suppressed panic.

Marcus buckled Lily into her car seat, and Ellie climbed into the passenger seat as they pulled away from the curb.

On the drive home, Lily chattered about the cookies, about a cartoon she'd watched, about the cat that lived in the complex and how Grandma said maybe they could get a cat too, could they get a cat, please, please, please?

"We'll see," Ellie said automatically.

"That means no."

"It means we'll talk about it when Daddy gets home."

The house felt hollow when they arrived. Marcus checked the locks while Ellie got Lily settled in the living room with crayons and paper.

"I'm going to start dinner," she told Marcus. "You're staying, right?"

"If you want me to."

"I do."

In the kitchen, she pulled ingredients from the refrigerator: pasta, jarred sauce, frozen meatballs. The kind of meal she'd have been embarrassed to serve a week ago.

Marcus leaned against the counter. "You remember Friday?"

"I remember the chicken."

"Derek said something about Thursday's board meeting—specific decisions that were going to be made."

"Well." Ellie stopped stirring the sauce. "Ben and Derek are both being considered for VP."

They stared at each other.

"That's a stretch," Ellie said after exchanging looks. "Even if Derek benefits from Ben going down, it doesn't make him a criminal."

"No, but it makes him someone to look at."

Ellie turned back to the stove, her mind spinning. Derek, setting up Ben. Derek, hiding evidence where it would be found. Derek, calling in the anonymous tip.

It seemed too calculated, too cruel.

But then again, she'd seen the way he looked at Ben during dinner—the casual condescension, the barely masked pleasure when he'd mentioned the promotion.

"I need proof," she said.

"Of what?"

"Something concrete, that Derek had the same hoodie."

Marcus pulled out his phone. "Social media. Derek's wife, Chelsea, is always posting. Maybe there's a photo."

They huddled over the phone, scrolling through Chelsea's Instagram—pictures of lattes, their renovated kitchen, Derek at a charity 5K last spring—

"There." Ellie pointed. "Zoom in."

The photo showed Derek crossing a finish line, arms raised. He wore running shorts and a gray hoodie, unzipped. The logo wasn't clear, but the style matched.

"Could be the same," Marcus said. "Could be different. Without seeing them side by side—"

"It's something," Ellie said. "A thread to pull."

From the living room, Lily sang to herself, a meandering tune about princesses and dragons.

Ellie closed her eyes and held tight to the sound of her daughter's voice, clear and sweet and unburdened by knowledge of what cruelty adults could inflict on each other.

Her phone buzzed again. Another unknown number.

This time, when she answered, no one spoke. Just breathing, low and steady, on the other end of the line.

"Hello?" Ellie said.

The breathing continued. Three seconds. Four. Then the call disconnected.

"Who was it?" Marcus asked.

"I don't know. They didn't say anything."

"Probably a wrong number."

"Probably."

But Ellie saved the number anyway, her thumb hovering over the screen. The silence of the kitchen pressed in around her—the hum of the refrigerator, Lily's cartoon voices from the living room, the ordinary sounds of her house that suddenly felt like they belonged to someone else's life.

CHAPTER 7

Tuesday morning

Ellie stood by the counter, watching the coffee drip into the carafe. She'd barely slept, Marcus's words cycling through her mind—thoughts that opened new possibilities, new hope.

The question was how to approach the problem. Right now, she only had loose suspicions, hardly something she could take to the police without being dismissed. No, she needed something more concrete. And she had to be careful.

The exhaustion dragged at her, a weight behind her eyes from the sleeping pill she'd taken hours ago. Its effects still clung to her, making her movements slow, her thoughts sluggish. But an uneasiness had driven her from bed before dawn—a vague dread that wouldn't let her rest.

She'd checked on Lily first, standing in the doorway of her daughter's room in the gray light. The girl slept soundly, Mr. Pemberton the stuffed elephant tucked under her arm. For now, the harsh realities of life hadn't penetrated Lily's consciousness. For now, she could sleep unburdened by the events that might soon rob her of security. For now, she could dream of a daddy who would return from his "business trip" with presents.

But how long could the truth be hidden?

The coffee maker sputtered its final drops. Ellie reached for a mug, her hand trembling slightly from fatigue, when the radio news bulletin cut through the morning haze.

"...police have confirmed the identity of the Heron Marsh suspect as 37-year-old Ben Carlson. While the suspect maintains his innocence, sources say investigators have recovered incriminating physical evidence from his home. Police have refused to comment on the nature of the items found..."

Ellie gripped the counter. It was out. His name. The privacy they had clung to was gone.

The sound of a key scraping in the front door lock stopped her heart. Metal sliding against metal. The door swung open with that familiar creak, but now the sound felt wrong, invasive. Footsteps in the hallway, heavy enough to hear, light enough to be uncertain.

Ellie's lungs seized. Every muscle in her body locked rigid. She couldn't move, couldn't think beyond the primitive surge of terror flooding her nervous system. Who had keys? Her mother. Just her mother. But her mind spiraled—what if it was Ben? What if someone else had a key? What if—

The footsteps drew closer to the kitchen doorway. Ellie stared at the empty space, waiting for a shape to fill it, her vision tunneling. She became acutely aware of how exposed she was, how vulnerable. The radio still murmured behind her, broadcasting Ben's name to the entire house.

The footsteps passed the kitchen without pausing, headed for the stairs, going up.

To Lily.

The realization hit like ice water. Ellie's paralysis

broke, but before she could move, before she could scream, she heard it—light, purposeful, familiar. Her mother's gait. Grace going up to check on Lily.

Grace turned, caught her eye, and called from the hallway: "Are you up already, Ellie?"

Ellie rushed to turn off the radio, her hands unsteady. The button stuck. She jabbed at it twice before the voices finally cut off, leaving only silence and the pounding of blood in her ears.

"You should have tried to sleep longer," Grace said, appearing in the doorway. "I thought I could take care of Lily since you have other things on your mind."

Her mother's voice reached her like a faint, distant murmur from which comprehensible words only gradually emerged.

"Why aren't you listening, Ellie? I've asked you twice now if you want me to take Lily to preschool."

"Preschool...?" Ellie looked at her, confused. She hadn't thought that far ahead. But it wasn't hard to imagine the looks the other mothers would give her, the whispers behind her back, the indignation and the pity.

Ellie declined her mother's offer. She needed time to think through the situation in all its terrible dimensions, and she could only do that alone. Grace stiffened at the blunt message that she might as well go home, her lips pressing into a thin line as she snatched her purse from the counter.

"Well, if you don't need me, I suppose..." Grace said, her voice trailing off. She gathered her purse from the counter, but her eyes stayed on Ellie. "Are you sure you're all right?"

"I'm fine, Mom. Thank you for coming over. Really."

"You don't look fine."

Ellie forced a smile. "Just tired. You know how it is."

But Grace wasn't fooled. Her daughter wasn't acting like herself—the trembling hands, the distraction, the way she'd jumped when the door opened. Something was wrong, something more than grief and exhaustion.

"I can stay longer if—"

"No, you've done so much already." Ellie moved to embrace her mother, holding on perhaps a moment too long. "I just need some time. With Lily. Just the two of us."

Grace pulled back, studying her daughter's face. "If you need anything..."

"I'll call."

After her mother left, Ellie stood at the window, watching the car pull away. The street looked normal—quiet, suburban, safe. But she knew better now. Word would spread. It was already spreading. Soon, everyone would know: the preschool teachers, the other mothers, the checkout clerks at the grocery store.

She couldn't let Lily face that. Not yet.

When she told her daughter she was staying home from preschool, Lily's face scrunched in confusion.

"But I don't feel sick," she protested. "I feel fine. See?" She jumped up and down to prove it.

Then her expression changed. Her eyes widened and a knowing smile spread across her face, as if she'd suddenly understood a wonderful secret.

"You think I can't guess? Daddy's coming home— we're going to pick Daddy up from the airport!"

Ellie knelt down to Lily's level and took her small hands.

"Sweetheart, no. Daddy isn't coming home today."

"Tomorrow?"

"Not tomorrow either. Daddy has to stay away for a while longer."

Lily's lower lip trembled. "But why? He said he'd bring me a present."

"I know, baby. But sometimes grown-up things take longer than we expect."

"How much longer?"

Ellie's throat tightened. "I don't know. Maybe a very long time."

Lily's face crumpled, and she burst into tears. "That's not fair! I want Daddy!"

Ellie pulled her close, absorbing the shuddering sobs against her chest. "I know. I want him home too."

Another dark cloud would darken Lily's sky that day. After several hours of begging, Ellie gave in to her pleas and let her go outside to play.

Ellie stood at the kitchen window, watching Lily crouch in the garden, arranging pebbles in careful rows. Ava from next door appeared at the fence, leaning over to whisper something. Ellie saw Lily's hand freeze mid-motion. The pebble dropped. Lily's whole body went rigid, and then she was running—stumbling—toward the house, her face twisted in a way Ellie had never seen before.

The back door burst open. Lily stood there, chest heaving, tears streaming down her flushed cheeks.

"What's wrong, sweetheart?" Ellie asked, alarmed. "Did someone hurt you?"

Lily's mouth opened, but only a strangled sound came out. She launched herself at Ellie, her small fists clutching fabric, her face buried against her mother's stomach.

"What happened? Lily, talk to me."

"Ava said—" The words came out in hiccups. "She said my daddy isn't on a trip. That he—that he's the bad man from the park. The one who hurts people."

Ellie felt her legs go weak. She sank to her knees, pulling Lily tight against her.

"That's not true, baby. Ava doesn't know what she's talking about."

"But she said everyone knows! She said it was on the news!"

Ellie had to put Lily to bed. The shock had triggered a fever, and it took much comfort and many soothing words before the girl finally drifted into a sleep-like trance.

Just as Ellie was heading down from the bedroom, the doorbell rang softly. She hesitated. Should she answer? It couldn't be Marcus—she knew he was busy all day. Who else? Will...?

Her stomach turned at the thought of Will. Was it possible he'd dare come back with new threats?

The bell rang again, and after a moment's consideration, she opened the door. To her surprise, she found Derek outside, half-hidden behind a giant bouquet of flowers.

"Ellie!" he said, holding her hand a moment too

long. "I know flowers can't comfort you on a day like this, but—"

"Do you want to come in?"

"Thanks, but I don't have much time."

He crossed the threshold anyway, though he declined to take off his coat—a dark blue parka with large pockets that Ellie remembered he'd been wearing that Sunday morning when he'd come over with some tools Ben was borrowing.

"I'm sorry you had to leave so quickly yesterday," he continued in a hushed tone. "I wanted to talk to you. To say how sorry I am that it wasn't Ben but me who—"

"You're sorry?" Ellie said. "You have no reason to be."

"Yes, I do! Ben would have been the obvious choice for section chief if it weren't for—"

He broke off and changed tracks.

"It's insane," Derek said, pacing the rug. "The cops are desperate. Arresting a guy like Ben over a tip-off? Because of some hoodie in the basement? It's flimsy, El. I've known Ben forever—longer than you have, in fact."

"I know. I've never seen Ben in a hoodie. Maybe you have? You've known him longer. I remember seeing an old photo of you in a gray hoodie—on Chelsea's Instagram."

For a second, Derek looked like he'd been struck, and he went pale. Then he recovered himself.

"Right," he agreed with a strained smile. "I'd almost forgotten. That was back in my carefree youth."

Ellie watched him closely. Not without a certain satisfaction, Ellie noted Derek's pallor beneath his tan.

He shifted, repeated a couple of times that he had to go, then slipped away.

Ellie frowned and thought intensely. There was something he'd said that didn't add up. She knew it was there but couldn't quite grasp it.

She tried calling Marcus, who didn't answer. Instead, she went upstairs to check on her daughter. Lily was sleeping, but her sleep was restless, and Ellie didn't dare turn on the light.

The darkness and fatigue must have made her doze off, because she suddenly jerked awake and looked around the now pitch-black room. And as if sleep had sharpened her memory, she knew what had puzzled her earlier.

It was Derek's words: *"Because of some hoodie in the basement."*

How did he know that? She hadn't said anything. The police hadn't released that detail—the radio had specifically said they refused to comment on the nature of the items found. The only people who knew about the hoodie were the detectives, Ben, and Ellie herself.

Unless Derek had put it there.

The situation became even more frightening if you followed that line of thinking. Then Derek emerged as a sexual predator and child abductor.

The thought was so monstrous she tried to push it away. But it kept returning, insistent. Derek had access to the house—he'd borrowed tools from Ben's workshop just last month. Derek benefited from Ben's arrest more than anyone. And Derek had shown up the very next morning, watching her with those flat, assessing eyes, pretending to offer sympathy while probing for information.

She needed to talk to someone. She needed to talk to Marcus.

Now she had to reach Marcus! But he still didn't answer, which surprised her—a couple of hours had passed since her last attempt.

While she stood with the phone in her hand, she heard footsteps outside the house. She tried to pierce the dusk with her gaze but only glimpsed a man's figure approaching with quick, almost running steps.

Her breath stopped. Her fingers went numb around the phone. What if Derek realized he'd given himself away and had come back to silence her?

Something hot and sharp flared in Ellie's chest, burning through the fear. Anger. Pure, clarifying anger. Someone had come to her house—to her home where her daughter rested upstairs. No. She wasn't going to cower inside while some stranger lurked in her yard, doing god-knows-what on her property.

Her hand was already on the doorknob before she'd fully decided to move. She yanked the door open, ready to shout, to demand answers.

But no one was there. She saw the gate slam shut, heard footsteps moving away, and everything was quiet again. On the doorstep lay a white envelope. On the front, written in large, block letters:

MRS. CARLSON.

With trembling hands, she tore open the envelope and found a single sheet of graph paper inside. The message was printed in generic block text, likely from a home computer.

YOUR HUSBAND IS INNOCENT. I HAVE PROOF. I WANT $25,000 AND YOU CANNOT GO TO THE POLICE. PUT THE MONEY IN YOUR DAUGHTER'S BACKPACK. SEND HER TO SCHOOL ON THURSDAY. WE ARE WATCHING. IF YOU GO TO THE POLICE—

The only part of the letter that was easy to read and coherent was the signature, printed in bold:

THE HERON MARSH PREDATOR.

* * *

Not until nine o'clock that evening did Ellie manage to reach Marcus by phone.

"I was just about to call," he said. "I haven't had time before now. Just got home. Has something happened?"

"Can I come over? I want to show you something."

"Well—" Marcus hesitated, clearly reluctant to have company. "I'll come to you instead. Is it good news or bad?"

"I don't know yet. I got a letter, a very strange letter. I'd appreciate it if you could look at it."

"Okay. I'll leave right now."

Ten minutes later, he was there. Ellie saw him coming, let him in, and thrust the letter into his hand without preamble. He studied it for a long time before slowly setting it down.

"Well, what do you think?" Ellie asked when he said nothing.

"Do you think it's real? That it's actually him who wrote it?"

Nothing else had occurred to her.

"He has proof," she pointed out weakly.

"Could just as easily be a scam. Someone who knows who you are and wants to exploit your difficult situation to trick you out of money under false pretenses."

Ellie felt a surge of anger. Why did Marcus have to ruin everything just when she'd started to hope?

"But what if it actually is real?" she objected. "Then it would be unforgivable if I did nothing. Maybe I can borrow the money from my mother."

She'd originally planned to ask Marcus for help, but she'd have to drop that idea.

"What about the other conditions? You can't go to the police—"

"I have no intention of doing that," she said.

"Use your head," Marcus said. "He's demanding that Lily take the money to school in her backpack— that you send her knowing someone is watching. Are you really going to let her do that? Wouldn't that be tempting fate?"

She had no answer for him. In her eagerness to help Ben, she'd overlooked how risky this was.

"And what guarantee do you have that he'll actually provide this so-called proof—whatever it is—after he takes the money?"

She couldn't argue anymore. Couldn't even point out that she naturally intended to watch over Lily.

"Sleep on it," Marcus advised seriously. "In the morning, you'll understand how right I am. You can't let yourself be frightened into rash actions. And now,

Ellie... unfortunately, I have to go. To tell you the truth, I have a guest waiting."

He made an apologetic gesture, said a hasty goodbye, and returned to his car with long strides.

Only after Marcus had left and Ellie stood upset and confused in the living room again did she notice the flowers Derek had brought.

Derek! In her confusion, she'd forgotten to tell Marcus about his visit and the strange remark he'd made. The letter had overshadowed everything else— and maybe she'd remembered wrong. Maybe she herself had at some point mentioned to Derek or Chelsea that the police had found the hoodie in Ben's basement.

But no. The news had been clear. The police refused to comment on the evidence. Derek shouldn't have known.

The day's many events had given her a pounding headache, and she took a pill, though she doubted it would help as long as problems kept overwhelming her. She brought the letter upstairs to the bedroom and read it several times before turning off the bedside lamp.

Imagine, if one day she could go to the police with proof that would demolish their idiotic theories!

CHAPTER 8

Wednesday

Marcus had advised her to sleep on it. Sleep she had—poorly. And the headache was still there when she woke to find it was five-thirty in the morning. Anxiety drove her from bed, and the first thing she saw in the downstairs hall was Lily's small red backpack.

She took it down from the hook. Did she dare take the risk? There was still time to consider. The deadline was set for tomorrow at noon.

But first, she had to get the money. What would her mother say when she came asking to borrow such a large sum?

She filled the coffee maker with water, measured out the grounds, and pressed start. The machine gurgled to life as she went upstairs to get dressed but was called into Lily's room by a frightened little voice.

"Mommy," Lily said, looking at her with wide, anxious eyes. "Is Daddy in a prison cell deep underground—like the dungeon in that movie we watched?"

"No, Lily, no! That was long ago. People who are in jail today live in proper rooms. Sort of like you and me."

"Then Daddy can come home if he wants?"

"Maybe. But he won't. Then the police would really think he's the bad man."

"They already think that."

"Yes. In a way, Lily, but—"

Ellie's sense that the child's curiosity wouldn't be easily satisfied would prove correct. The questions came in waves. But in between, the girl sat huddled in a corner, brooding while despair and confusion played across her small face.

And through it all, one thought kept circling back to Ellie, sharp as a knife: *How did Derek know about the hoodie?*

The phone rang at ten-thirty.

"I'm sorry about last night," Marcus said. His tone was stiff, but he didn't hang up.

Ellie stared at the kitchen counter where the ransom note still lay, its words burned into her memory.

"It's fine."

"You're not actually considering meeting this person's demands, are you, Ellie?"

"No."

The lie emerged smooth and complete. She had already decided—she would pay. She would handle this alone and accept the consequences.

"Good." Relief flooded through the phone. "Then you'll turn the letter over to the police?"

"Of course."

Another lie. The police would set a trap. Whoever sent that note would vanish, and the promised evidence would disappear with them. Worse, they might decide the letter was a forgery—something she'd manufactured herself to deflect suspicion from Ben.

But Marcus wasn't convinced. He spent another twenty minutes extracting promises that she wouldn't let herself be manipulated by an anonymous letter. During the entire conversation, Ellie's mind worked through a single problem: how to get twenty-five thousand dollars.

When she finally ended the call, she sat motionless at the kitchen table. Twenty-five thousand dollars. An impossible sum.

She tried her mother first.

"Twenty-five thousand?" Grace's voice climbed an octave. "That's... Ellie, that's a fortune. What on earth do you need that much for?"

Ellie had prepared for the question. She'd decided against mentioning the letter.

"It's for Ben, Mom. I can't explain right now."

"Sweetheart, I wish I could help. I really do. But with the special assessment the condo board just levied, and the property taxes coming due, I simply don't have—"

Her mother continued talking, but Ellie stopped listening. She had to find another way.

The jewelry box sat on her dresser where it had always been. Her grandmother's pearls. The diamond earrings Ben had given her on their fifth anniversary. Her engagement ring—she slipped it off her finger and held it up to the light. Two carats. How much was that worth now?

The pawnshop on Miller Street gave her four thousand for everything. She'd expected more, but the man behind the counter had looked at her with knowing eyes, and she'd been too desperate to negotiate.

The joint savings account was frozen—the police had seen to that. But her personal checking account, the one she'd kept from before the marriage, still had eight thousand in it. Emergency money. This qualified.

That left thirteen thousand.

She called Marcus back.

"I need to borrow money," she said, the words scraping her throat raw. "Thirteen thousand dollars."

A long pause. "Ellie, what is this really about?"

"Please, Marcus. I wouldn't ask if I had any other choice."

She heard him exhale slowly. "This is about the letter, isn't it? You're going to pay."

"Will you help me or not?"

Another pause, longer this time. "I'll have it for you by tomorrow morning. But Ellie—this is a mistake."

"Thank you," she said, and hung up before he could say anything else.

* * *

Thursday morning dawned gray and thick with fog. Ellie counted the bills three times—twenty-five thousand exactly—and placed them in an envelope. The ransom note had specified the red backpack, the bench near the playground, noon.

She couldn't bring Lily. The thought of taking her daughter anywhere near that park, near whoever had written that note, made her physically ill. But the alternative—leaving Lily alone—was equally impossible.

Mrs. Patterson next door had watched Lily before. She was retired, kind, and had grandchildren of her own.

"Just for an hour or two," Ellie said, forcing a smile as she walked Lily across the lawn. "Mommy has an errand to run."

"Of course, dear." Mrs. Patterson's weathered face creased with concern. "Is everything all right? You look pale."

"Fine. Just tired."

Lily clung to Ellie's hand. "I want to come with you, Mommy."

"Not this time, sweetheart." Ellie knelt down and kissed her daughter's forehead. "You play with Mrs. Patterson. I'll be back before you know it."

She watched Lily wave from the doorway, that small hand rising and falling, until she couldn't see it anymore.

The fog had not lifted since dawn; it was dense and impenetrable. Now, at noon, visibility extended no more than thirty feet. Ellie walked the familiar path through Heron Marsh with determined steps, the backpack heavy on her shoulder.

Her palms were slick with sweat. Every shadow in the fog looked like a figure waiting, watching. The back of her neck prickled, and she kept glancing over her shoulder at shapes that dissolved into mist when she looked directly at them.

She felt calm as she approached the playground, the envelope of cash heavy in the backpack, but the sensation of being watched—that prickling awareness between her shoulder blades—refused to fade. She stopped on the path and turned around.

No one. Just shapes in the fog, indistinct and shifting.

The church bell began its noon toll.

Ellie placed the red backpack on the designated bench. Her hands trembled. Her shirt stuck to her back despite the October chill.

Then she retreated to the thick cluster of rhododendrons nearby and crouched behind them. She had chosen well—the bench remained visible through the gaps in the branches. Now she would wait and watch what happened next.

Minutes passed. The fog swirled. No one came.

Footsteps crunched on the gravel path behind her. Terror shot through her. She spun around.

A tall figure emerged from the fog, moving with long, purposeful strides.

Her mind went blank. Run? Scream?

Then she recognized him.

"Marcus!" Relief and anger collided in her chest.

He looked equally startled.

"I called your house about twenty minutes ago," he said. "When you didn't answer, I knew you'd come here anyway. Ellie, how could you? At least you had the sense not to bring Lily—"

"She's at Mrs. Patterson's," Ellie said. "I'm not completely reckless."

But even as she spoke, a cold dread was settling into her stomach. Something was wrong. She could feel it, the way you feel a storm coming before the first thunder.

"The backpack," she said suddenly, lurching toward the bench. Had someone already retrieved the money?

Her hands shook as she unzipped it. The envelope was still there, every bill accounted for.

They stared at each other, confusion replacing tension for a single moment. Then they heard it—the whisper of bicycle tires on wet pavement.

A woman on a bike materialized from the fog.

"Excuse me," Marcus called out. "Have you seen anyone near this bench in the last few minutes?"

The woman shook her head. She hadn't seen anyone.

"Wait—there was a man. Young. But he was alone. I'm certain of that."

Ellie's phone rang. She fumbled it from her pocket.

"Mrs. Carlson?" Mrs. Patterson's voice was thin, stretched tight with worry. "I'm so sorry to bother you, but I can't find Lily anywhere. She was playing in the backyard, and I went inside to get her some juice, and when I came back—"

"The gate was open," Mrs. Patterson said, the words rushing out like she couldn't stop them. "And her elephant—Mr. Pemberton—it was still on the chair. She didn't take it with her."

The world contracted to a single point of white-hot terror.

"What do you mean you can't find her?"

"I've looked everywhere. The yard, the house, up and down the street. She's just... she's gone."

* * *

Marcus drove. Ellie couldn't. Her hands were shaking too badly, and her vision kept tunneling until she had to put her head between her knees.

Mrs. Patterson stood on her porch, tears streaming down her face. "I only looked away for a minute. Just one minute."

Ellie ran through the house, through the backyard, screaming Lily's name until her throat was raw. The back gate hung open—she was certain Mrs. Patterson had closed it.

"Help me, Marcus." Ellie's voice cracked. "Please help me."

His face had gone pale, his expression grim.

"There's only one thing to do. We go to the police."

Ellie nodded, grateful he wasn't berating her for ignoring his warnings. She couldn't allow herself to think about what might be happening to Lily. Couldn't let her mind form the words: what if the Heron Marsh Predator has her now?

Marcus put his arm around her shoulders.

"Come on," he said, his voice steady. "Let's go. Together."

A patrol car was dispatched to the neighborhood, followed by a second, and finally a K-9 unit. Reports went out to the detectives who had spent months investigating the string of assaults believed to be the work of a single perpetrator.

"Mrs. Carlson." A familiar voice cut through the chaos. "We've met before."

Detective Reyes stepped out of an unmarked sedan.

"Your daughter is missing." He paused, consulting his notepad. "Tell me exactly what happened, from the beginning."

He doesn't believe me, she realized with mounting horror. He thinks I staged this—that I'm trying to help Ben somehow.

Before she could respond, the K-9 officer approached.

"Rex picked up a scent from the backyard," he reported. "But the trail ends at the curb. Someone put her in a vehicle."

Reyes nodded, his jaw tight. He turned back to Ellie, his gaze sharp and searching.

"Mrs. Carlson, I need to inform you that your husband may be relevant to your daughter's disappearance."

The implication hit Ellie like ice water. Ben. He thought Ben had taken Lily.

"That's impossible. You have Ben in custody. How could he possibly—"

"Was in custody," Reyes interrupted, his emphasis razor-sharp. "We were transporting him to the crime scene for a walkthrough when he escaped. He pushed past an officer and fled into the marsh."

The words didn't make sense. Ellie heard them, but they seemed to come from very far away, muffled by the roaring in her ears. Ben escaped. Lily gone. The two facts collided in her mind, and she saw exactly what Reyes was thinking.

"No," she breathed. "No, Ben wouldn't—he loves her more than anything—"

Ellie turned to Marcus, desperate for an anchor. He stood frozen, his face ashen, and she saw her own horror reflected back at her.

"This wasn't Ben," she said, her voice climbing. "I have proof—I received a letter—"

"What letter?"

The words tumbled out now, unstoppable. The ransom note. The demand for twenty-five thousand dollars. The promise of evidence clearing Ben's name.

Reyes's expression shifted from skepticism to barely contained fury. "You received a letter from someone claiming to be the predator and you didn't report it?

You brought twenty-five thousand dollars in cash to a meeting with this person?"

"He said he was being watched. That if I told anyone, he'd disappear and Ben would be convicted. I—" Her voice broke. "I just wanted proof. I wanted my husband back."

"Show me this letter."

"It's at my house."

He pulled out his radio. "I am regrouping to the Carlson residence to retrieve some evidence. And expand the search perimeter—check all roads leading out of town."

Marcus grabbed Lily's backpack from where Ellie had dropped it. "Look at this." He yanked it open, revealing the stacks of bills. "Twenty-five thousand dollars. She wasn't lying about the ransom. Someone set this up."

Reyes stared at the money, then at Ellie. Something shifted in his eyes—not quite belief, but the beginning of doubt in his own theory.

"If there's a letter," he said slowly, "if someone really did contact you claiming to be the predator... then your husband escaping today, your daughter disappearing today—that's not a coincidence."

"You think someone planned this," Marcus said.

"I think we need to find your daughter." Reyes's hand moved to his radio again. "All units, be advised: we are treating this as an abduction. Suspect may be the individual known as the Heron Marsh Predator. Victim is a five-year-old female, last seen wearing—" He looked at Ellie.

"Pink jacket," she whispered. "Pink sneakers. Her hair is in pigtails."

As Reyes relayed the description, Ellie stared at the fog still swirling around them. The ransom note. The money in the backpack. The emptiness where Lily should have been.

"You think he took her," she said. "Ben."

Reyes lowered the radio. His face was unreadable.

"I think we have two possibilities, Mrs. Carlson. Either your husband escaped custody and abducted your daughter, or there's a predator out there who's been playing all of us from the beginning." He paused. "Either way, your little girl is in danger. And right now, we don't know where either of them are."

The fog pressed in around them, cold and suffocating. Somewhere out there, in that gray void, Lily was waiting. Scared. Alone.

And Ellie had no idea who had taken her.

<h1>CHAPTER 9</h1>

Thursday afternoon

Detective Reyes' voice cut through the chaos, issuing commands to officers, redirecting the search, deploying resources. Ellie watched from the doorway, numb, as patrol cars scattered in new directions and the K-9 unit was loaded back into its van.

Lily's description went out over police radio—a small girl, five years old, brown hair in pigtails, pink jacket with unicorn patches. Ellie had sewn those patches herself. Her hands had been steady then.

Now they trembled.

"Mrs. Carlson." Reyes gestured her inside. "We need to go over this again."

The kitchen table became command central. Maps spread across the surface where Ellie had served breakfast that morning—a lifetime ago. Officers debated scenarios in clipped tones. One suggested Ben might have taken Lily through the rail system, could be halfway to Connecticut by now. Another disagreed. If the girl knew her father, trusted him, she'd go willingly. They wouldn't attract attention.

"What about the money?" Ellie forced the words past the constriction in her throat. "Someone sent that note. Someone wanted me at the park."

"To get you away from your daughter." Reyes' jaw tightened. "Question is whether your husband orchestrated it from inside, or—"

"Ben didn't do this." Marcus spoke from the

doorway. His face was drawn. "I'm going with the search teams. I know Lily better than officers working off a description."

Reyes studied him. After a moment, he nodded.

As Marcus turned to leave, a patrol officer burst through the door. In his gloved hand, he held a small white mitten sealed in a plastic bag. His face was flushed from running.

"Found this at the edge of the parking lot. Dog led us there before losing the scent."

The air in the kitchen turned thin, insufficient. Ellie stared at the lavender thread on the mitten—recognized it instantly. A loose loop near the embroidered flower. Her mother had knitted them last Christmas. If she pulled that thread, the whole thing would unravel. Just like everything else.

"Easy." Reyes kept his voice steady. "We're going to find her."

But his voice had lost its earlier conviction. They both knew what that mitten meant—dropped in haste or pulled off in struggle, evidence of a trail now lost.

"I need to do something." Ellie gripped his arm. "I can't just sit here."

"You can help by talking this through." Reyes pulled out a chair. "Tell me again about the neighbor. Mrs. Patterson. How long was Lily in her yard?"

"Ten minutes. Maybe fifteen."

"And Mrs. Patterson saw nothing?"

"She was inside getting them juice. She looked out the window and Lily was gone."

One of the officers spoke up. "We canvassed the street. Nobody saw a vehicle, but with the fog—"

"Someone had to see her." Ellie's voice rose. "A five-year-old doesn't just vanish. There are houses everywhere, people, cameras—"

"We're checking doorbell footage now." Reyes kept his tone measured. "But Mrs. Carlson, you need to prepare yourself. The predator's pattern has been to approach children in isolated areas. If he took Lily in broad daylight from a residential street, he's escalating. That suggests—"

"Don't." The word came out sharp. "Don't tell me what it suggests."

Reyes' radio crackled. He listened, his expression shifting. He spoke into it, rapid-fire questions. Then he turned to Ellie.

"We got a hit. A shop owner on Falkner Street noticed a girl matching Lily's description about an hour ago. She was holding hands with a local business owner: Edwin Thorne."

Ellie was already moving. "I know that name—the toy store in the old part of town."

"Thorne's Toy Box." Reyes grabbed his keys. "I'm driving."

* * *

Falkner Street looked like something from a different era. The buildings leaned together, brick facades stained and crumbling, windows dark behind metal grates. The fog had lifted, but the narrow street remained shadowed, caught between taller structures on either side.

"There." Marcus pointed from the back seat.

The storefront was narrow, squeezed between a shuttered insurance office and a pawn shop. THORNE'S TOY BOX, the faded sign read. The window display held vintage toys—tin robots, wooden puppets, porcelain dolls with glassy stares.

The lights were off. A handwritten sign hung in the door: CLOSED.

Reyes parked at an angle, blocking the entrance. Two patrol cars pulled in behind them.

"Stay in the vehicle," Reyes told Ellie.

"No." She was already out, slamming the door.

Reyes tried the handle. Locked. He knocked, waited five seconds, knocked harder. Nothing.

"Police! Open the door!"

Silence answered him.

One of the officers spoke into his radio, requesting information on the building's layout. Ellie pressed her face to the glass, cupping her hands against the reflection. Inside, she could make out dim shapes—shelves, a counter, boxes stacked against walls.

No movement. No Lily.

"There's an apartment above." Marcus had walked to the corner and was looking up. "The entrance might be around back."

They followed him into an alley thick with the smell of garbage and old grease. A metal door, painted gray, had the number 68 stenciled on it. Reyes tried the handle.

It opened.

The stairwell beyond was dark and narrow, walls pressing in on both sides. The smell was worse here—

mildew and something else, something sweet and rotting.

Reyes drew his weapon. "Mrs. Carlson, you need to wait outside."

But she was already pushing past him, taking the stairs two at a time. She couldn't wait. Every second Lily was with that man was a second too long.

"Lily!" Her voice echoed up the stairwell. "Lily, honey, it's Mommy!"

A sound above them—a door slamming.

Then footsteps, running, descending fast.

Reyes shouted something, but Ellie didn't hear. She was climbing, her legs burning, her breath ragged. The footsteps grew louder. Someone was coming down toward them.

They met on the landing between floors.

A man—tall, thin, his face gaunt in the dim light. He pulled up short when he saw them, his eyes going wide. For a frozen moment, nobody moved.

Then he tried to push past.

Reyes tackled him. They went down hard, the man's skull cracking against the concrete step. He thrashed beneath Reyes, making sounds—not words, just sounds, animal-like and panicked.

"Where is she?" Reyes had him pinned, one knee on his back. "Where's the girl?"

The man was sobbing now, his thin shoulders heaving. "She was lonely! She was just lonely! I just wanted to help her—"

Ellie didn't wait to hear more. She scrambled past

the tangle of limbs, boots slipping on the slick concrete, and hauled herself up to the landing.

The apartment door stood open at the top of the stairs. A visiting card was tacked to the frame: K. Thorne. Below it, in childish writing: Edwin.

The smell hit her first—stale lavender masking the copper tang of old plumbing. The apartment was a tomb of cardboard boxes. Her voice died in her throat.

A rustle of fabric.

She saw the curtain—a length of faded velvet hung across the far wall, separating off a small alcove.

Dear God, help me. Don't let me be too late.

Ellie tore through the velvet curtain.

Eyes. Hundreds of them. Porcelain, glass, painted. They lined the shelves from floor to ceiling, a silent audience in Victorian lace—baby dolls with rosebud mouths, antique dolls in faded dresses. They sat on shelves, stood on the floor, hung from hooks on the wall.

And in the center, curled on a daybed like just another doll in the collection, was Lily.

Still. Too still.

"Lily?"

The small chest hitched. A breath.

Ellie fell to her knees, the impact jarring her teeth, but she didn't feel it. She gathered the small, warm body against her chest, holding her so tight the child squirmed.

Lily stirred, stiffening. "Mr. Edwin? Did you bring the bears?"

"No, baby. It's me."

Lily blinked, her eyes unfocused. "Mommy? Is the bad man gone?"

The relief hit like a physical force. Ellie was crying—deep, shuddering sobs that she couldn't control.

Lily wriggled in her arms. "He said to wait." Her voice was thick with sleep. She clutched a large porcelain doll, nearly her own size. "He went to get the candy. He said I have to be quiet so I don't wake the other babies."

She looked at the wall of dead, glass eyes. "I don't like them, Mommy. They stare."

Footsteps on the stairs. Reyes appeared in the doorway, his weapon drawn, his face tense. When he saw them, his shoulders dropped.

"She's okay?"

"She's okay." Ellie couldn't stop touching Lily—her hair, her face, her small hands. Checking that she was real, solid, safe.

Ellie carried her daughter past Reyes, down the narrow stairs, out into the alley where more police cars had gathered. Marcus stood by the door, his face drawn. When he saw Lily, he closed his eyes.

"Thank God," he whispered.

An officer tried to stop Ellie to ask questions, but Reyes waved him off. "Give her a minute."

Ellie sat in the open door of the patrol car, Lily on her lap. She couldn't let go. Couldn't stop shaking.

"Mrs. Carlson." Reyes crouched beside them. "I need to ask Lily a few questions. Is that alright?"

Lily looked up at him, her eyes curious but unafraid. "Are you a policeman?"

"I am. My name is Detective Reyes." He lowered his

voice. "Can you tell me how you got to Mr. Thorne's apartment?"

"We walked. I saw him outside Mrs. Patterson's house and he said would I like to see his toy store? And I said yes because Mommy takes me there sometimes. Mr. Thorne is nice. He always lets me hold the toys."

"Did you go into the store?"

"No. He said it was closed today. But he said I could come upstairs and see his special collection." Lily's face fell. "I told him my daddy was away on a work trip, and he started crying. That's when I felt scared."

Ellie's arms tightened around her.

"But then he gave me the doll and said I could take a nap if I was tired, and he'd go get gummy bears from the candy lady. And I did get tired, so I laid down." Lily twisted to look up at Ellie. "Did I do something wrong? You look upset."

"No, baby. You didn't do anything wrong." Ellie buried her face in Lily's hair. The scent of her—sweet and clean—cut through everything else.

Reyes straightened. "We've got officers bringing Thorne down now. He's confessed to everything—the approaches in the park, the assaults, all of it."

"What about Ben?" Marcus asked.

"Armed units are still searching, but—" Reyes paused as his radio crackled. He listened, his expression shifting. "Copy that."

He turned to Ellie. "They have your husband."

"Where?"

"Highway patrol picked him up two miles from here. He was on foot, trying to cut through the woods to get back to the house. He fought the officers—screaming that he had to find his daughter."

Lily perked up. "Daddy's back? Can we see him?"

"Soon, honey." Ellie pressed her cheek to the top of Lily's head. "Soon."

But Reyes was still watching her, and something in his face made her stomach clench.

"There's something else." He spoke quietly. "Your daughter said she saw someone else. Before Thorne found her. A man who smelled like beer. He tried to grab her."

Ellie went cold. "What?"

"I ran away," Lily said matter-of-factly. "I ran and ran and then Mr. Thorne was there. He said 'what's wrong, little one?' and I told him about the scary man. So Mr. Thorne said he'd keep me safe."

"Did you know the man?" Reyes asked.

Lily shook her head. "He smelled sour. Like that stuff Daddy drinks from the brown bottles. And he had a spider on his hand."

Ellie froze. Will had a tarantula tattoo on the web of his thumb. She had stared at it when he grabbed her wrist in the driveway.

Marcus swore under his breath.

"We'll find him," Reyes said. "But right now, let's get you and Lily to the station. You'll want to see your husband."

They drove through streets that looked familiar but strange, as if Ellie had been gone for years instead of hours. The fog had burned off completely. The sun was setting, casting everything in orange light.

Lily chattered in the back seat about the dolls, about Mr. Thorne's sad face, about whether she could bring the big doll home. Ellie listened without really hearing. Her mind was stuck on one thought: *Lily was safe. After everything, Lily was safe.*

But the relief was tangled with something else—horror at what might have happened, fury at Edwin Thorne, at Will, at whoever had planted that hoodie in Ben's workshop, at herself for leaving Lily with a neighbor while she chased a ransom demand.

She'd made so many mistakes.

"We're here," Reyes said.

The police station looked different now—less threatening, more utilitarian, just a building, just brick and glass and fluorescent light.

Inside, the chaos had subsided. Officers moved with purpose but without urgency. Someone had brought coffee and donuts. The smell made Ellie's stomach turn.

"Mrs. Carlson." A female officer approached. "Your husband is in Interview Two. Would you like to see him?"

Lily grabbed her hand. "Can I see Daddy?"

The officer smiled. "Of course."

They followed her down a hallway, through a door, into a small room with a table and chairs. And there was Ben—thinner, exhausted, a bruise blooming across his left cheekbone, but alive, real.

"Daddy!" Lily launched herself at him.

Ben caught her, buried his face in her hair. His shoulders shook. "Oh God. Oh God, Lily."

Ellie stood in the doorway, watching. She should

go to him. She should fall into his arms, complete the reunion. But her feet wouldn't move.

Ben looked up at her over Lily's head. His eyes were red, his face hollow.

"I'm sorry," he said. "Ellie, I'm so sorry. When I heard the radio call—your address, a missing child—I lost my mind. I couldn't just sit there in handcuffs while our daughter—"

His voice broke.

"That's how you heard?" Ellie asked.

"The officers' radios. They were transporting me to the crime scene for some kind of walkthrough, and the call came through. I just—" He shook his head. "I had to get to her. I wasn't thinking about consequences."

And she believed him. She believed he hadn't taken their daughter, hadn't hurt those children, hadn't done any of the terrible things he'd been accused of.

But watching him hold Lily, something shifted in her chest. They weren't finished. The nightmare wasn't over. Someone had framed him, and until they knew who and why, none of them were safe.

Reyes appeared beside her. "We need to talk about next steps. Thorne's lawyer is already here. He's going to claim diminished capacity—says his daughter died twenty years ago and he never recovered. The judge might show leniency."

"He took children," Ellie's voice was flat. "He terrified them."

"I know. But mental illness complicates things. He'll be institutionalized at minimum, probably for life. That's something."

"And Ben?"

"The evidence against him is circumstantial with Thorne in custody. But we still need to figure out who planted those items in your house." Reyes studied her. "You said your husband's coworker, Derek Thornton, knew details about the evidence that weren't public?"

"Yes. He said, 'some hoodie in the basement.' The radio specifically said police weren't commenting on the evidence."

"We need to speak with him."

Ellie nodded. Through the doorway, she watched Ben whisper something to Lily. Their daughter giggled—the sound bright and normal, impossibly precious.

"Mrs. Carlson?" An officer poked his head into the hallway. "Your mother is here, and someone named Marcus Webb. They're asking to see you."

"Send them in, please."

She stepped into the room. Ben looked up, his eyes meeting hers. There was so much to say, but Lily was there, safe between them, and for this moment that was enough.

Grace appeared in the doorway, gasping when she saw Lily. "Oh thank God. Oh, my baby girl."

Lily wriggled out of Ben's arms and ran to her grandmother. "Nana! I got to see a whole room full of dollies!"

Marcus waited in the hallway, giving the family space. When Ellie's eyes found his, he offered a small nod. I'm here. Whatever you need.

Reyes cleared his throat. "I'll give you folks some time. But Mr. Carlson, you'll need to stay here until we sort this out. Breaking out of custody carries serious consequences. But given the circumstances—your daughter's disappearance, Thorne's confession—the DA might show leniency, especially since no one was seriously hurt."

"I understand." Ben's voice was hoarse. "I just needed to know she was safe."

"We're going to find who did this," Reyes said. "The frame job, the evidence planting—we'll figure it out."

He left, closing the door behind him.

In the sudden quiet, Ellie sat beside Ben. Lily climbed into her lap, yawning. The adrenaline was wearing off, leaving exhaustion in its wake.

"I should have fixed that gate lock," Ben said quietly.

"This isn't about the gate." Ellie watched Lily's eyes drift closed. "Someone did this to you. To us. And I'm going to find out who."

Ben took her hand. His fingers were cold. "I thought I'd lost you both."

"You didn't." She squeezed back. "We're still here."

But as she held her sleeping daughter and her husband's hand, Ellie knew the hardest part was still ahead. Someone had orchestrated all of this—the planted evidence, the ruined reputation, the stolen week of their lives. Someone had set Ben up to take the fall for Edwin Thorne's crimes.

And that someone was still out there.

Chapter 10

Thursday night

Two hours later, Reyes found her in the station's break room, nursing a cup of cold coffee while Lily slept in Ben's arms on a worn couch.

"We picked up your cousin," he said quietly, pulling out a chair across from her. "William Garrett. Bus station in Hartford, one-way ticket to Miami in his pocket."

Ellie's hand tightened on the cup. "Will took Lily?"

"Not exactly. But he tried." Reyes pulled out his notepad. "We found a typed copy of that ransom letter in his bag. He confessed to writing it—said he saw an opportunity when Ben was arrested. Figured you'd be desperate enough to pay."

"The twenty-five thousand dollars." Ellie felt sick. "He was going to take the money and disappear."

"That was the plan. But when you didn't leave the backpack unattended, he improvised. Saw Lily alone in Mrs. Patterson's yard and thought he could grab her." Reyes shook his head. "She was too fast for him. Ran straight into Thorne's arms."

"So Will didn't actually take her."

"No. Thorne did that on his own. Your cousin's facing extortion charges, attempted robbery, maybe attempted kidnapping, depending on how the DA wants to play it." Reyes paused. "He won't be bothering your family again for a long time."

"What about the money?" Ellie asked. "The twenty-five thousand in the backpack."

"Evidence for now. You'll get it back once the case is closed—probably a few months." Reyes gave her a tired smile. "Though I imagine you're not too concerned about that right now."

He was right. She'd have paid ten times that amount for the moment Lily opened her eyes in that horrible room and said, "Mommy."

Ellie looked at Will's face in her memory—the desperate eyes, the twitching hands, the way he'd smiled when she gave him money. "Family helps family," he'd said.

"Good," she said, and meant it.

"After your information about Derek Thornton's knowledge of the evidence," Reyes said, "we looked into how he could have known. Thornton called the station the morning after we searched your house. Claimed he was a concerned friend checking on the investigation's progress. The desk sergeant—a rookie, not following protocol—confirmed we'd recovered items matching the predator's description. When Thornton pressed for details, the sergeant mentioned clothing. Derek asked specifically: 'A hoodie?' The sergeant said yes before realizing he'd said too much."

Ellie felt sick. "So Derek was checking to make sure you'd found what he planted."

"Exactly. He needed confirmation the frame was working. We also traced the anonymous tip that started this whole thing. Burner phone, purchased with cash three days before Ben's arrest. Security footage from the store shows Derek buying it. He made the call Saturday evening, gave us just enough detail to establish probable cause for questioning."

Reyes nodded slowly. "We've been looking into the Thorntons. Turns out Chelsea volunteers at Riverside Behavioral Health—has for years. Crisis counseling, art therapy, that sort of thing."

"I know. She mentions it constantly."

"One of their long-term patients was Edwin Thorne."

The name hit her like ice water. "Edwin. The toy store."

"Chelsea had access to his case file, including detailed notes about his... approaches—what he wore, how he operated." Reyes leaned forward. "Six weeks ago, Derek Thornton purchased mirrored sunglasses from a sporting goods store in Providence. Paid cash, but the security footage is clear."

Ellie's coffee cup slipped from her fingers. She barely noticed the lukewarm liquid spreading across the table.

"Derek framed Ben."

"We believe so. He had motive—the promotion. He had means—access to your house through the spare workshop key. When he returned your husband's wrench, he planted the hoodie and sunglasses in the workshop cabinet Saturday morning. Then, that same evening, he called in an anonymous tip from a burner phone, told our tip line he'd seen someone matching the predator's description entering and leaving your property. That's what triggered our investigation and the warrant for questioning."

Ellie felt sick. Was all this for the VP position, the coveted corner office?

Reyes paused a moment before continuing. "He also lied to you about the Wednesday meeting. You asked him about it, correct? When it ended?"

Ellie nodded, remembering. "He said five o'clock. But Ben told me six-thirty."

"Security logs show they were both in the conference room until six forty-five. Thornton told you five o'clock deliberately—to make your husband's timeline look suspicious, to plant doubt, even with his own wife."

"But he didn't—he's not—"

"He's not the predator, no. That was Thorne, acting alone. But Derek saw an opportunity to eliminate his competition and took it." Reyes stood. "We're executing arrest warrants tonight. I thought you should know."

After he left, Ellie sat motionless, her mind reeling. Derek, who'd stood in her living room and offered condolences. Derek, who'd asked pointed questions about the investigation. Derek, who'd smiled at her across the dinner table while her husband sat in a cell for crimes he didn't commit.

She thought about the promotion Ben had wanted so badly, about the late nights and the stress and the way his face had gone tight whenever Derek's name came up.

It had all been for nothing—a competition that Derek had decided to win by destroying them.

Ben stirred on the couch, Lily still curled against his chest. He looked at Ellie, saw something in her face.

"What is it?"

"Derek," she said. "Derek planted the evidence. He and Chelsea—they knew about Thorne through her charity work. They set you up."

Ben was quiet for a long moment. When he spoke, his voice was flat and hard in a way she'd never heard before.

"I'm going to kill him."

"No." Ellie crossed to him, took his face in her hands. "You're going to watch him get arrested. You're going to watch him lose everything—his job, his reputation, his freedom. And then you're going to take that promotion and be better at it than he ever could have been."

Ben's jaw worked. She could see the rage in him, barely contained.

"And then?"

"And then we're going to go home. Lock the doors. Hold our daughter. And figure out how to be a family again."

He closed his eyes. When he opened them, some of the fury had drained away, replaced by exhaustion and something that might have been relief.

"Okay," he said. "Okay."

CHAPTER 11

Three Months Later — January

The gate latch was new—heavy-duty steel that required a key from both sides. Ben had installed it the week after he came home, along with motion sensors over the back door, a camera covering the driveway, and a new deadbolt on the basement that required a six-digit code. The old latch had never held properly; the warped wood kept working it loose. All those nights Ellie had found it open, convinced someone was watching them, and it had just been shoddy hardware all along.

"Overkill," Ellie had said, watching him drill holes in the fence post.

"Maybe." He'd kissed her forehead, sawdust in his hair. "But I sleep better."

She couldn't argue with that. They both slept better now, though the nightmares still came sometimes— Ellie dreaming of empty swings and open gates, Ben jerking awake convinced he was still in that cell, still waiting for news that would never come.

But the nightmares were less frequent. And in between them, there were good days. Days when Lily laughed at breakfast and Ben made pancakes in the shape of elephants and the house felt like home again instead of a crime scene.

Today was a good day.

Ellie stood at the kitchen window, coffee warming her hands, watching Ben push Lily on the new swing set. He'd built it himself over Christmas break—a proper one this time, with a slide and a climbing wall and a little fort at the top where Lily could hide with Mr. Pemberton and pretend to be a princess in a tower.

The old swing set was gone. Ellie had asked Ben to take it down the week after everything happened. She couldn't look at it without seeing that empty seat, that stuffed elephant slumped against the chains.

Her phone buzzed on the counter. A text from Marcus:

Jury's back on Derek. Guilty on all counts.

Ellie typed back:

Good.

Four simple letters that contained a universe of feeling. Relief. Vindication. And something darker—satisfaction, maybe, at the thought of Derek in an orange jumpsuit, stripped of his corner office and his country club membership and his smug certainty that money and connections could buy him anything.

The trial had been brutal. Derek's lawyers had tried everything—claimed the evidence was circumstantial, suggested Ben had planted the hoodie himself, even implied that Ellie and Marcus were having an affair and had framed Derek together. None of it stuck. The security footage from Providence was too clear. Chelsea's case notes on Edwin Thorne were too damning. And Derek himself had crumbled on the stand, his polished veneer cracking under cross-examination until he'd finally screamed that Ben didn't deserve the promotion anyway, that he'd earned it, that none of this would have happened if the board had just recognized his obvious superiority.

The jury had deliberated for four hours.

Now Derek was facing fifteen years for evidence tampering, filing false reports, and conspiracy. Chelsea would serve her eighteen months and probably write a memoir about it—*Standing By My Man: A Story of Love and Loyalty*. The thought made Ellie want to laugh and vomit simultaneously.

As for Will—he'd pleaded guilty to extortion and attempted robbery in exchange for a reduced sentence. Five years in federal prison, then supervised release. He'd sent Ellie a letter from his cell, rambling and self-pitying, full of excuses about his addiction and his childhood and how none of it was really his fault.

She'd burned it without finishing.

The back door opened, bringing a rush of cold air and the sound of Lily's laughter.

"Mommy! Daddy pushed me so high I could see Mrs. Patterson's roof!"

"That does sound high." Ellie scooped Lily up— she was getting too big for this, her legs dangling past Ellie's knees—and buried her nose in her daughter's hair. She still did this a dozen times a day, breathing her in, confirming she was real and solid and here.

Ben stamped snow off his boots and crossed to the coffee maker. He moved more easily now, the tension that had lived in his shoulders for months finally beginning to ease. Last week, the board had officially offered him the VP position.

The journey to that offer had been longer than either of them expected. The Thursday board meeting—the one that was supposed to decide everything—had been indefinitely postponed when Ben was arrested. The company couldn't very well promote a man in police custody, even if half the office whispered it was a setup.

For three months, the VP position sat empty. Derek had self-destructed spectacularly, and Ben was tainted by association—guilty by proximity, if not by deed. The whispers in the break room, the careful distance colleagues kept, the way conversations stopped when he walked past. Ben had returned to work after his release, but it had been hell.

His mentor had told him, "They're waiting to see if the trial exonerates you. If Derek was convicted, if it was clear he had been framed..."

And they had. The trial verdict came down on a Tuesday—guilty on all counts. By Friday, the CEO had called Ben into his office and said they owed him an apology, and that they should have seen through Thornton's manipulation, should have known Ben's character better.

Ben had sat across that massive desk, feeling that an apology didn't erase three months of hell. Didn't give him back the nights he'd spent in a cell. Didn't undo the look on his daughter's face when she'd asked if he was the "bad man."

But he'd accepted the apology anyway. Accepted the promotion. Because refusing would mean Derek had won something, even in defeat.

"Patterson's roof?" Ben raised an eyebrow at Lily. "I don't remember pushing you that high."

"You did! I saw the chimney and everything!"

"The chimney. Wow." Ben caught Ellie's eye over

Lily's head and smiled—a real smile, the kind that crinkled the corners of his eyes. She hadn't seen that smile in months.

"Daddy, can we build a snowman after lunch?"

"If you eat all your vegetables."

"Even the green beans?"

"Especially the green beans."

Lily made a face but didn't argue. She wiggled out of Ellie's arms and ran to the living room, where Mr. Pemberton waited on the couch. A moment later, Ellie heard her narrating an elaborate story about elephants who lived in snow castles.

Ben came up behind Ellie and wrapped his arms around her waist, his chin resting on her shoulder.

"Derek?" he asked, having seen her check her phone.

"Guilty. All counts."

He exhaled slowly. "Good."

They stood there for a while, watching through the window as snow began to fall—fat, lazy flakes that caught the light and sparkled like something from a fairy tale. The yard looked clean and white and new.

"I was thinking," Ben said quietly, "about this summer. Maybe we could take Lily somewhere. The beach, or the mountains. Somewhere far away from here."

"Running away?"

"Taking a vacation." He turned her to face him. "We've earned it."

Ellie thought about everything they'd survived: the arrest, the accusations, the days when she hadn't known if her husband was a monster or a victim, the hours when her daughter was missing and she'd bargained with a God she wasn't sure she believed in—anything, she'd promised, I'll give you anything, just bring her back safe.

"The beach," she said. "Lily wants to learn to surf."

"Lily wants to do everything."

Ben laughed—a real laugh, rusty from disuse but genuine. The sound made something loosen in Ellie's chest, some last knot of fear she hadn't realized she was still carrying.

They weren't okay yet. Not completely. There were still nights when Ben woke up shaking, still moments when Ellie's heart seized at the sight of an empty swing, still a wariness in Lily's eyes when strangers approached her at the playground.

But they were getting there. Day by day, nightmare by nightmare, they were finding their way back to something like normal.

And sometimes—like now, with snow falling outside, her daughter's voice floating in from the other room, and her husband's arms around her—sometimes normal felt like more than enough.

The gate latch gleamed silver in the winter light, secure and solid.

Ellie let herself breathe.

The end

Yesteryear's stories reflected today
Yabot AB
www.yabot.se/en

ALSO BY MATILDA HART

She had the perfect career. They had other plans.

When two mismatched guardian angels intervene in high-powered lawyer Elizabeth Thompson's life, she's forced to confront an impossible choice: the success she's built—or the dreams she buried long ago.

A heartwarming story of divine mischief, second chances, and finding the courage to color outside the lines.

The Angels' Canvas (print, e-book & audiobook)